BONE CARNIVAL

MEGAN LYNCH

To Marlowe
Stay kind, stay curious.

Megan Lynch

To Marlowe

Stay Kind, Stay curious.

Margfor

BONE CARNIVAL
MEGAN LYNCH

ORANGE
BLOSSOM
PUBLISHING

Maitland, Florida

Orange Blossom Publishing
Maitland, Florida
www.orangeblossombooks.com
info@orangeblossombooks.com

First Edition: October 2023

Library of Congress Control Number: 2023907153

Edited by: Arielle Haughee
Formatted by: Autumn Skye
Cover design: Sanja Mosic

Print ISBN: 978-1-949935-75-2
eBook ISBN: 978-1-949935-76-9

Printed in the U.S.A.

DEDICATION

To my students.
You are loved and treasured
beyond all understanding.

TABLE OF CONTENTS

Chapter 1 1
Chapter 2 10
Chapter 3 17
Chapter 4 28
Chapter 5 49
Chapter 6 59
Chapter 7 65
Chapter 8 74
Chapter 9 79
Chapter 10 88
Chapter 11 96
Chapter 12 101
Chapter 13 109
Chapter 14 111
Chapter 15 115
Chapter 16 121
Chapter 17 128
Chapter 18 136
Chapter 19 141
Chapter 20 148

Chapter 21 153
Chapter 22 159
Chapter 23 170
Chapter 24 176
Chapter 25 180
Chapter 26 188
Chapter 27 190
Chapter 28 199

Discussion Questions 209
Acknowledgements 211
About The Author 215

Mom says I'm a magnet for trouble. But here's the thing about magnets: they don't choose what they attract. So even if that's true, and I am a magnet, that doesn't really mean it's my fault, right?

But now, as men in sunglasses and suits stomp through our new apartment in their thick black boots, flipping open our suitcases, and running gloved hands over the walls and empty shelves, I'm starting to wonder if I'd be able to switch to being a magnet for literally anything else.

"Who even *are* these guys?" I whisper to my brother, Enzo. He's five years older, and he has the advantage of being able to speak Italian.

"*Agenzia Informazioni a Sicurezza Esterna.* Italian FBI." He rubs his forehead in an eerie impression of Mom. "Man, Mia, couldn't you have given us one day? It would have been nice to unpack before you set the law on our tail."

As Mom shows an officer her passport and letters from the University—my parents' employer for the summer—I can only imagine what she's saying in her clear, perfect Italian. *I'm so sorry about the mix-up. My daughter has an...overactive imagination.*

Now, just an hour after my fun encounter with our downstairs doorman, Mom appears on the threshold with her eyes narrowed into slits. "Mia. Would you mind telling these," she jerks her head, *"gentlemen* what exactly you told our doorman?"

An older man with a badge at his heart and two hairy thumbs tucked into his pockets glares at me.

"And why?" Dad adds.

I take a deep breath. If I sound sorry enough, maybe he'll just go away, and Mom and Dad can start to forget about this.

"I...kind of implied we were spies, and our passports were fake, and we were bugging the lobby. I was bored, but I'm sorry. I was just joking with him. I didn't think he'd take me seriously. I'm just a kid!"

"Signore Russo says your daughter, eh, talked differently?"

Dad rolls his eyes. "Mia likes to do accents."

"I can do lots of them!" I say, but when they all three—Mom, Dad, and this *Agenzia* guy—shoot identical disapproving looks at me, I frown and look at my shoes again. "I mean, I was just talking like the bad guys on *Rocky and Bullwinkle.* It's this vintage TV show I have on my tablet. I didn't know I would scare him so much."

Mom closes her eyes and pinches the bridge of her nose.

"Signore Russo was not scared of you, little girl," says the agenzia man in English. I assume my parents have told him that I'm the only one in the house who can't speak his language. They tell everyone. "He had a concern, and he did his duty by calling us to investigate. No more games like this, yes? Games, jokes, this *Rocky and Bullwonky—*"

"Bullwinkle," I interrupt without thinking.

His cheeks flush. "Whatever. They're for your playmates, *capisci?*"

I nod. Capisci means understand, which I've known since I was three, but almost nobody asks it sincerely. Grown-ups use it as a finishing touch on their lectures, a way to tell you *I'm tired of yelling at you now, just shut up and be good already.* I've heard it from my mom and dad a million times, but this is the first time anyone outside of my family has used it. Is it his job to come out here and confirm that we're not a family of spies, or to lecture me? And *what* playmates? I've been in Rome for three hours, and nobody ever wants to be my friend for too long anyway. But I know what I have to do now: I slump my shoulders forward and stick out my lower lip, as if I'm very sorry for having lied to the gullible doorman.

He's still glaring at me, so I let that lip quiver, and he frowns and turns away. That's when I know he's about to back down. He turns to my parents. "I have a granddaughter like this," he says in English, probably for my benefit. "It takes some time for children to learn. No harm done."

"Thank you, signore," says Mom.

As he turns back to talk to my parents, I notice he's set his little notebook down on the kitchen table. With all of them distracted, I see my chance, and take it: I gingerly slip it into the waistband of my leggings. Even if I can't read everything, I'd still like to see what he wrote about us. I'll just use Google translate and see what I can put together.

All of the officers file out the front door. I purposefully keep my eyes on them until the door finally shuts. The moment it does, the air in the room feels thick, awkward, and exasperated. I try to lighten the mood.

"I thought Rome was supposed to be a big city. Doesn't the Italian FBI have better things to do than to throw us a welcome party?"

Mom breathes sharply out her nose and rubs the space between her eyebrows, her lifelong signal of impatience with me. "Mia Elizabeth Moretti," she says with a slight pause between each part of my name, "didn't we *just* have a talk about cutting back on these antics?"

We did. Back home, in Louisville, my family has somewhat of a reputation for causing trouble. Or rather, I have the reputation. It's not like I go seeking it out though, and half the time, it's for a good reason, and *some* of the time, I don't even get caught.

"Should we really classify this as an *antic,* though?" I ask. "Why would he have called the police, anyway? Shouldn't he have known better than to trust a—"

"Pathological liar?" my brother finishes for me, smirking.

I pretend I didn't hear that. "I'm just saying that, obviously, if you two were international spies, I would not be the one to trust with that information. I'm twelve!"

4

"Twelve is old enough to know not to joke like that around people," says Dad. "If you were six, that would be one thing. We'd put the story on Facebook, and people would laugh about it. But twelve? Mia, you're just too old for this. And yes, this was absolutely an antic."

With my tongue, I prod at my loose tooth. Everyone keeps saying things like this: you're too old for this or that, whatever I happen to like, and I can't seem to grow up fast enough for anybody. "I'm sorry," I say.

"Just go to your room and unpack your clothes," says Mom. "You too, Enzo. Let Dad and I get settled in."

"But I didn't do anything!" Enzo says, looking up from his phone.

"You should have kept an eye on her while we were trying to get the key!" Dad says. "If you'd taken more responsibility with your sister..."

I leave them to have the same old familiar argument—*it's Mia that made all the trouble, Enzo is saying again, don't blame me!*—and disappear into my room. For a second, I'm afraid it'll turn into something like The Big Fight, but the raised voices die down after a few seconds when Enzo slams his own door. Now that we're all in separate rooms again, just like we usually are back home, my shoulders droop heavily downward.

No.

I won't let us go back to this. Not this soon into the summer, anyway. I will be good.

My room is small, with a twin bed in the corner and a wardrobe with a broken hinge, so that one of the wooden doors hangs lopsided. There's a tiny bedside table just big enough for the miniature lamp that sits on it. Dust and scratches bespeckle the formerly-white walls. It'll definitely do for the summer, but right now, it's just too small for my feelings. There's a window with no curtains that opens up onto a fire escape.

I sit with my back against my bedroom door and take out the chief's notebook. I flip through it for a moment. All in Italian, just as I suspected. There's a sketch of a little boy here, next to the words *carnival strano*. I pull up the translation app on my phone and hover the camera lens over the words. The English appears on the screen: *strange carnival.* Weird. Maybe his son got ahold of it and drew a picture of himself or something. I keep flipping through, and on the last page, I do see my name written, Mia Moretti. It's an Italian name since both of my parents are Italian. It's been their dream to come here to work for years and years. Remembering this makes my stomach churn with guilt.

I will actually try harder. No more telling stories to people just for fun. Getting in a little trouble with the local police is one thing, giving the embassy a reason to send us back to the US is another. I put the notebook in the wardrobe and stack a few clothes on top. *Be good, be good, be good.* This shouldn't be too hard.

The notebook is hidden well. We'll be here for three months, and I swear to myself it'll be the only stolen item in my room all summer. I am *going* to be good. For real.

I decide to take a little break from unpacking and open my window to crawl out onto the fire escape. The evening air feels a little sticky, a little heavy, and I can smell the fire and garlic from the cafe below where

6

people sit at tables on the sidewalk in front of their dinners. My room feels confining, but the fire escape seems small in a good way—a little safe spot in the vastness of Rome all around me.

On the plane, I watched *Roman Holiday* on this app called Old Hollywood that has all these classic movies and TV shows. Audrey Hepburn is a princess on tour in Rome and is sick of everyone else making decisions for her, so she runs away and explores the city. It's really old, though—it was made in the '50s, and even though it sounds kind of ridiculous, I sort of wonder how much of that Rome is still here today. I'd kind of love to run away, just for a day, and maybe get a secret haircut like the undercover princess. Maybe even meet a friend—people in movies never go on those adventures alone. Maybe I'll meet someone who actually wants to explore here, not like the boring, scaredy-cat girls back home who bail at the first warning from the mall security guard.

A little voice inside me—my conscience, maybe?— reminds me of my goal: *be good.* But I think I could still be good and figure out how this fire escape works. I search with my fingers along the iron, experimenting with what moves easily and what doesn't. There has to be a way to climb all the way down to the street.

Suddenly the ladder below screeches and swings. I jump with fright, but the platform I'm sitting on stays steady.

"Grrr-oul?"

A skinny cat is on the top rung of the ladder which is swinging down beneath me. There's a white star on his chest, and one of the toes on his front paw is white, but other than those patches, he is jet black. He's looking up at me with big green eyes, asking for help without words.

"Oh," I say involuntarily. I've never held a cat before. My parents won't let us have a pet. The only cat I've ever really known is my aunt's, who is fluffy and blond and mean. Because of that, I don't want to reach out my hand.

"Come on," I say, my voice high like I'm talking to a baby, "you can do it. Jump up."

He doesn't move.

"Are you scared? Do you need help getting up?"

He purrs and—I swear—shakes his head *yes.*

I stop and consider. He seems nice enough, and if he's not, cat scratches heal eventually, I guess. I reach down and scoop him up, feeling his scrawny ribs in my palm. He goes limp but doesn't take his eyes away. When he's safely next to me, I withdraw my hand, but this guy is nothing like the razor-clawed monster at Aunt Tiffany's house. He rubs against my leg in thanks.

"Nice to meet you," I say and scratch the top of his head. He purrs and blinks at me three times, slowly and affectionately. Then he drops down beside me, belly-up, and purrs like he's turned his internal volume up to ten.

Okay, so now I'm in love. I know Mom and Dad won't let me keep a cat, but it's not like they're here to see him, and neither is Enzo. He rubs his face against my palm, and I make a mental note to ask for some tuna fish when we get groceries. It's not long before he's in my lap, chin against my knee, purring like I'm his new best friend. I take one of his black paws in my hand and squeeze gently.

"You can stay with me as long as you want to out here," I tell him, reaching for his other paw. "Are you lonely too?"

As soon as my fingers touch his other paw—the one with the white toe—he abruptly jumps out of my lap and gives me an angry look.

"What'd I do?" I ask. He jumps up the ladder and then onto the platform above me. He stops there and stares at me without blinking. Apparently I can't make anyone happy today.

A noise from inside makes me turn back toward the window.

It's Mom's phone, ringing again. The thought passes in my head so quickly—the notebook—when the question is answered, in the form of Mom's sharp exhale and her sharper voice:

"*Mia!*"

2

Okay, now, for sure, I am going to be good. Like, starting right now.

I kind of have to, because Mom and Dad are actually really mad at me for the whole stolen notebook thing. Mom even walked me to the station where I had to give old Signore Hairy Thumbs yet another apology. I thought it might even kind of be nice to walk down there, just the two of us, but she was not in the mood to make the best out of a bad situation. And I was really hoping that once we got to Rome things would change.

In my imagination, I'd seen us walking around together, shopping and eating interesting food, being more like a TV family and having fun together. In *I Love Lucy,* Lucy gets to smash grapes with her feet to make wine in Italy—I think I'd be good at that. Or maybe even riding in a gondola! Or, wait, that might only be in Venice.

But instead of any of that all I get for days is a lot of lectures about how I need to settle down and follow directions. I'd really like somebody to talk to, but Enzo only wants to talk with his friends back home on his phone, and there's nobody else here.

The only one who pays any attention to me at all is this stray cat. Now that I'm stocked up on cans of tuna, he likes me even more. It's weird, but he seems to know exactly when I'm at my loneliest too—like on Sunday morning, when I lie in bed for way too long because I have the feeling that even if I get up, nobody will talk to me anyway. That's when I hear the scratch on the glass and the dull sound of his furry body thunking against the window. I give him some food and water and smile as he settles next to me, looking out across the rooftops.

"I kind of wish I was a cat too," I tell him. "Then I could come with you, instead of—"

"Mia!" Dad calls through my door. "Get ready. We're going to church."

As if he understands, the cat rises, stretches, and walks away.

I should name him. He seems like he already has a name, though, and he just can't tell me.

I meet my family outside just as the car arrives to take us to Mass at a big church called St. Peter's Basilica. It's in this special little city-state called The Vatican, where the Pope—who is basically the king of the Catholic church—lives. The driver drops us off a few blocks away from it, and as we get closer, the whole place so big that I have trouble getting grounded--everywhere I look is marble and cut stone and life-sized statues of saints. Though it's early, there are hordes of people in a gigantic square in front of the church. Some of them are dressed really funny. I recognize the nuns, but there are guards at the gates that are dressed in balloon-like pants with orange-and-purple stripes. They're carrying some sort of medieval weapon, and the looks on their faces suggest that they know how to use them.

"Who are those guys?" I ask.

"The Swiss Guard," says Dad. "They're like the Vatican's army. They protect the area."

"Why would the Vatican need an army? Are they Swiss, or are they Italian? And why are they dressed like extras on *The Hunchback of Notre Dame*?"

"Mia, just keep your eyes open and your mouth closed," says Dad, squeezing my hand and lowering his voice as we walk inside the church. "That's what I always do in a new country, and I'm always glad I do."

"But I can open my eyes and mouth at the same time," I tell him.

He frowns. "That's not what I meant. I mean, listen more than you speak. You don't always have to be the most interesting person in the room."

I want to tell him that I can't help being the most interesting person in the room, but I can tell that won't go over well.

It's not my fault that most people are so boring. Most of my friends back home—when they're still hanging out with me—would rather scroll mindlessly and look at memes they're going to forget in five minutes than actually do something—anything!—that scares them even a little. It's not hard to be the most interesting person in the room when all the rooms are filled with people like Harper Fergeson, who said she was up for saving the lobsters in the tank at the mall, and who cried when we got caught and told the security guard it was all my idea. So what if it was? It's barbaric to keep lobsters in a tank in the front lobby of a mall restaurant for people to pick out and eat. I told her so, but she said she still didn't want to be around me anymore, and then she started ignoring my texts. Fine by me, I say. She's so boring. She's more boring than an entire church service in Latin, and I should know; I sat through an entire one, wondering whether the Swiss Guard are just there for show or if they could actually beat someone up without ruffling their bloomers.

After church, a woman approaches us with a stack of papers. She says something to my parents in Italian and tries to give them one of the papers, but they wave their hands, pretend they don't speak Italian, and keep walking.

Since I'm behind them, I can see the look on her face as they go on. She looks so sad that I reach my hand out.

"Per Favore." It's one of the only words I know. It means please.

She gives me a grateful look and hands me a poster with a little boy's face on it. He's about my age with wavy hair and thick eyebrows. The girls back home would call him cute. The woman pats my cheek and her touch makes me think maybe she's his mother—I've seen mothers do that before, though mine does not. She holds my gaze for just a second before leaving to distribute the rest of her flyers. I get out my phone and google the word on top in bold letters. When the result loads, I gasp.

Missing.

13

We go to a restaurant for lunch, because as cranky as Mom and Dad still are about the whole theft-from-the-police-chief incident, they're still excited for pizza. This is more like it.

I say *grazie* to the waiter when he arrives at the table.

Mom and Dad smile noncommittally. Enzo snorts.

"That means *thank you,* genius, not *hello,*" Enzo says, leaning across the red-checkered tablecloth as he flicks a lock of hair from his forehead.

"I know what it means," I say, gritting my teeth. "I was telling him thank you for coming to the table. He appreciated it. He smiled."

"He was laughing at you because you said thank you when you should have said hello."

"Mom, how do you say 'I want a new brother' in Italian?"

She shrugs and picks up the one menu the waiter left at our table. "You can learn it for yourself at language camp."

"Language camp?"

"You and Enzo are both going. It starts the day after tomorrow."

Enzo looks up, his eyes wide under his long bangs. "But it's summer!"

"And?" Mom asks.

"And I already know Italian! And I'm seventeen!"

"There's always room for improvement. And you're still a child."

14

"We're supposed to be on vacation! You're the ones who are here for work, not us!" I cry, suddenly on Enzo's side.

"You are on vacation."

"You're making us go to *school*." Enzo says.

"Not school. Camp."

We both know what her kind of camp is. "Camp" is a word that implies firewood, tents, woods, and peeing behind a tree. But since we were toddlers, Enzo and I have been going to very different kinds of camps—math camp, science camp, computer-coding camp. It's all school, but with the most hardcore kids from every district. There are grades and tests and everything. We've never been camping for real in our lives.

Our waiter arrives with some sparkling water, and another behind him hefts a huge pizza on his shoulder. When he puts it down, it's round with sauce and cheese, but there are no slices. It's not cut.

"*Grazi*," Mom says, at a proper time and in a proper accent, and the waiter smiles again and leaves without saying anything.

"What are we supposed to do?" I ask. "Eat it like dinosaurs?"

"Exactly," says my dad. He roars and tucks his elbows back behind his ribs to make little T-Rex arms. In a raspy voice he says, "Hunting for prey is overrated! Dadnosour hungry!"

Mom rolls her eyes, but I spread my arms like a pterodactyl and snap my jaw open and shut a few times. "I'm a pizzasaurus predator!" I screech.

Dad and I chomp at the air while Enzo tries to shrink himself down and disappear inside his hoodie.

15

I giggle at Dad and then look to see if Mom's smiling too, and stop. I lower my arms.

She's looking down at her screen and pointing her phone at us. When I stop, she and Dad grin at each other. Dad stops instantly, his playful silliness gone as quick as it came, and starts to cut the pizza into triangles as she taps her screen to upload the video she just took of us. I unroll my silverware from my napkin, feeling stupid. I should have known. I thought we were just having fun, but it was all for Instagram.

3

The next day, I keep scratching at my throat where a ruffle sits unnaturally at the high-necked tank top my mom bought me before we left Louisville. She told me it was specifically for this event—a welcome dinner for new faculty—and called it a "blouse." I'm sure she bought it thinking it would look good in pictures. Even though we just got here, I'm already dying to take it off.

"Just keep your hands away from your throat," says Mom out of the side of her mouth.

"I can't," I tell her.

She sighs. "Why not just look for our table? There's the list."

I scan the giant list, labeled *Welcome, International Faculty!* There are lots of names and numbers underneath, but it's all alphabetical, so I find us pretty quickly: *Moretti, Drs. Sarah and Andrew, and family, table 6.*

Enzo takes one look at the tables and groans. "This is going to be one of those dinners where we have to talk to strangers, isn't it?"

I see what he's talking about: the tables are circular and huge. There'll be more people there than just our family. "They'll get bored quickly," I say. "It'll be, 'how's school, are you looking forward to Italian camp,' and then they'll go back to talking about research."

Enzo's mouth twitches. "If we're lucky. Remember that time we got stuck with the kindergarten teacher?"

"Dr. Terry is a professor of children's literature," interrupts mom. "And she was very interested to talk to you both."

Enzo and I both smirk as I remember Dr. Terry asking us in her cartoon-character voice what our favorite books were, what the main character's journey was like, and whether or not we "connected" to it.

On our way to the table, I see another girl about my age. Unlike me, she doesn't seem to have any siblings around. She stands with her arms crossed, waiting for her parents to stop talking. She has on the same high-necked blouse as me! I guess our moms saw the same Instagram ad. I squint at her across the room to examine it—yep, it's the same, except hers is purple and mine is red.

She catches me staring. Instead of looking away, I smile and wave. She doesn't react; she only turns her head back to the boring conversation she looked like she was trying to avoid. I frown.

"Who is that?" I ask Mom.

"If you want to know, go introduce yourself," Mom says. But we've arrived at table six, and the chairs and tables are squeezed so close together that I wouldn't be able to go without it being very obvious that I was making a beeline for her.

"That's okay," I say. "Maybe I'll meet her later at Italian camp." I pick up the folded program and start to read it, but it's all in Italian. "When does it start again?"

"The day after tomorrow," says Mom. "9:00 a.m."

The program starts with two old men speaking at a microphone: one in Italian and the other translating in English. It's nothing too groundbreaking: "Welcome, we're very delighted to have you, we are embarking on an exciting new school year," et cetera. I scratch my neck. I use my tongue to wiggle my tooth. I drink all my water, which is easy to do since it doesn't have any ice in it to slow me down.

"Mom," I say after all the water in my glass is gone, "I need to go to the bathroom."

She glances around and points to a sign with the outline of a woman in a dress. I back my chair up exactly one inch—all that the space will allow—and slide out, squeezing around men and women who make annoyed noises at having to move their bodies at all.

When I finally make it out of the sea of purple tablecloths, I notice something square and small by the wall. Without thinking much about it, I pick it up. It's a little clutch purse, small but expensive looking. I'll give it to someone in charge when I'm done in the bathroom. I take it into the stall with me.

Peeing feels like sweet freedom after being cramped and crowded and bored. So good, in fact, that I take the opportunity to unbutton the collar of the blouse too. And then that feels so good that I decide to go ahead and investigate the contents of the purse.

The ID is an American driver's license from New York. The woman in the picture looks like smiling is not her favorite activity; even her eyes look stern. I feel like I should get her together with my mom. They could be friends and bond over a shared passion of never having any fun.

There's some cash in the wallet, which I ignore, and a pearl bracelet at the bottom of the clutch, which I slip around my wrist. Like the clutch itself, it feels weighty and pricey. There's a delicate little gold tag that sticks out slightly from the pearls; it says something I can't read but I assume is a fancy brand. I pretend I'm on the red carpet, giving an impromptu interview to the press about my latest movie. I pretend the flapping neckline of my shirt is some new style that I'm making wildly popular right now and wave to the imaginary cameras. I pose, moving my eyes from right to left to give each of the photographers in line a good shot of me.

"Miss Moretti, it's time to go into the theater now," I imagine my manager saying, and with that, I open the stall door with a flourish, the hand with the bracelet on it outstretched and purposeful, step out, and freeze.

The girl is standing there in front of the sinks, arms crossed over her purple shirt. One of her perfect eyebrows is raised at me.

"What are you doing with my mom's purse?"

"What, this?" I say. I maintain eye contact, but I can feel the heat rising around my eyes. "This is my purse."

"No, it's not. And that's my mom's bracelet too. Give it back."

"Don't you want me to wash my hands first?"

She steps aside, and I scrub for a long time, careful not to get any water on the pearls. I ask myself why

I told her the purse was mine, but I have no answer. I just said it without thinking. Better just to come clean, I guess.

I dry my hands and hand her the bracelet and the purse. "I'm sorry. I just saw it sitting there with nobody around, and I was going to turn it into someone after I went to the bathroom. I promise."

She ignores me, unzipping it and looking inside. "Did you take anything?" she asks.

"No."

"Why should I believe you? You just lied and said it was yours."

I grin. "Why did you ask, then?"

She doesn't answer, but twists her face in an expression I've seen before. It's an expression that says *I don't like you,* or *I don't trust you,* or *you are bad.*

I don't like it. I've never liked it. In Louisville, this expression usually means that yet another one of my friends has realized that I'm no good for them, that they'll eventually just get in more trouble if they keep hanging out with me, and drop me for someone else. It's why I don't have a best friend. It's why I can usually make friends quick, but can't keep them. I've never seen it this early on though.

I'll make it right. I'll make her like me.

"Look, this is no big deal. I was going to give it back, I swear. I was just curious, you know? Haven't you ever wanted to know what other people think is important enough to carry around with them?"

But she stiffens, not taking the bait.

"And it's really pretty too," I'm blurting now and talking way too fast. "It looks like something Audrey

Hepburn would wear in an old movie. Have you seen *Roman Holiday?*"

"I'm going to ask my mom if anything is missing, and if anything is, I'm going to tell her you took it." She pivots and storms back out to the crowded banquet hall.

I start to look at myself in the mirror, but when I catch the sight of my own eyes, I look away. I button the back of my blouse and think about how much better she looks in hers than I do in mine. In my mind, I can see the two of us on the red carpet, under the heading WHO WORE IT BEST? Her. Whatever her name is, she's best. I hear my mother's voice in my head: *What is wrong with you?*

Suddenly I cannot stand to be alone anymore. I go out to be with my family. I'll be nice to Enzo—he's usually nice back when he knows I really need it.

Like when I was four, my parents gave me a card for my birthday, but no present. They told me they'd given some money to my college fund, and I'd thank them later, but I was still crushed, because I didn't know what college was back then, and all the kids on TV *always* got presents for their birthdays. Parties too.

The next day, I saw a water gun in Target and asked Mom if it could be my birthday present instead. She said no, but I couldn't let it go—it was big and pink and green and I knew I'd be perfect for watering tree-tops in the neighborhood. When she said no again, I cried and cried and reminded her that my birthday was yesterday, and she hadn't gotten me a present. Enzo stood up for me, telling Mom that I had a point. When he said this, a few other shoppers slowed their carts to look at us, and feeling their eyes on us made me cry more. Mom snatched the water gun, tossed it in the cart, and paid for it at check out. I was elated until we got into the car. She put it in the trunk as I buckled myself in the booster seat. I asked Mom if I could play with it soon, and she replied that I wouldn't be playing with it at all—she bought it to stop me from crying and drawing attention to ourselves, but she planned to return it to the store later. She and Daddy had put almost two hundred dollars into my college fund; plastic toys only lasted a few months, and so I should be grateful, she said.

I'll never forget that. I didn't even cry. I just felt like my heart was going to melt away from my ribcage and form a puddle under my feet. Enzo was there, though— he put his arms around me and didn't let go.

The next afternoon, Enzo beckoned me into the hall, then pointed at my room. I looked, and the water gun was sitting on my bed, new in its package. "Just play with it while Mom and Dad are at work," he told me, "and keep it under your bed the rest of the time." So I did. Later, I found out he'd asked a neighbor to drive him to the store and bought it for me with his own money. That water gun was our secret the entire summer, until it got confiscated by our babysitter when our neighbor complained that the water was making streaks on her window. I'd been trying to clean them.

Enzo has gotten more into his phone this year and only talks to me when he has to. I thought maybe he'd talk to me more after The Big Fight, but that didn't happen. But I'll tell him I need him, and he'll be there for me. I know it.

The purple tables are now laden with little plates with bread and cheese and salad on them. At my place, no one has given me any food yet, and Enzo is tearing into his dinner roll.

"Did they say they'd come back?" I ask.

"You can have some of mine," says Enzo, and he gives me half of his roll.

I sigh and take it, but I don't really want it; I wanted someone to make sure I had my own. Suddenly I don't want to talk to Enzo after all; I just want to forget what happened in the bathroom. My parents are talking to the other adults.

"And you?" someone across the table is asking my mom. "Where are you from?"

"Andy and I are from Pennsylvania, but we've lived in Louisville for about ten years now. We're both at the university there. It's a nice city, but *so conservative.*"

I've heard her say that before. I don't really know what it means, but I know it's not something she likes. Maybe she thinks I'm conservative.

Dinner is served, and I am impressively (I think) well behaved throughout the entire affair. I am so proud of myself that I start looking around the room for that girl again, wondering if she's keeping her eye on me. If so, I wonder if she sees that I ordered water with no ice instead of juice or chocolate milk, like I wanted to. Would she give me credit for eating all of my salad? When I finally catch sight of her, and her back is to me, I am disappointed. Not even Dad notices what a great job I'm doing, sitting quietly and drawing no attention to myself.

When the dinner is over, we walk outside, Enzo and I shuffling awkwardly behind Mom and Dad onto the brick walkway. My parents are invited out for more wine by our table mates. Mom glances my way and shakes her head.

"The kids aren't really mature enough to be by themselves just yet," she says.

"We've left them alone before," Dad protests, but it's weak, and I think it's because he's remembering what happened last time he left us alone. Enzo and I tried to cook a fancy dinner instead of eating the leftovers they told us to finish, and we ended up melting the cutting board and breaking the oven. We tried to clean it, but we were still hungry, so we ordered pizza and then kind of forgot. I think they were angrier about having to throw the leftovers out than they were about the burnt-plastic smell that we couldn't get rid of.

"Another time," Mom says with authority.

I'm feeling disappointed when I see that girl and her mom walking toward us. I take Mom's hand and squeeze it. "I'm tired," I say without looking back. "Can we go home now?"

"Sure, honey," says Mom. "I'm tired too."

She and I walk away at a steady clip toward our apartment while Enzo and Dad trail behind. Just when I think I can start feeling safe, we hear a voice behind us, an American woman's, say, "Excuse me!"

For a split second, I don't think Mom hears, and I'm going to ignore her, but when she stops, I close my eyes and swallow. *Here we go.*

"Hi," says the woman, completely ignoring me and addressing my mom. "I just wanted to introduce myself. I'm Trisha James, your new colleague in the economics department."

"Oh, yes!" Mom's tone shifts immediately to her public voice—warm and friendly. Nothing like a fellow economist to set her at ease. Her daughter is behind her, looking very interested in a trashcan—which is more like just a suspended trash liner halfway filled with water bottles and empty gelato cups—on the sidewalk.

"I saw you and your husband have children too. I'm glad Grace will have a friend. Are they signed up for language camp at the university?"

"They are." Mom squeezes my shoulder as if we're close. "Mia is really looking forward to it."

"Grace too," says Trisha James, and she gives her daughter an appraising look. "We hired an Italian tutor to help prepare her for this a year ago, but it didn't do much good. She doesn't have much of an aptitude for language."

Grace looks down at her shoes now and kicks a pebble into the gutter. A wave of pity washes over me; at least my mom has the decency to pretend she likes me in public. I wonder why Grace followed me into the bathroom at all—I have a feeling if I had to live with this lady, I'd definitely watch someone steal her purse and stay to savor my dinner.

"Hopefully it'll be a fun experience for them," says my mom and turns to Grace. "Are you coming with your mom to orientation tomorrow? Mia and Enzo will be there. Maybe you and Mia could play together."

"She'll be there," says her mom, "but she'll have lots of work to do. She keeps busy!"

"Well, we'll see you tomorrow, then. Have a good night!" says my mom, and we start to walk away again. I'm so relieved to have gotten away that I actually let out a breath I didn't know I was holding.

"Oh, Mia?" calls Trisha James from behind us.

My heart stops.

"Thank you for finding my purse."

I nod as a response, my cheeks burning and my fingers tightening around Mom's hand. Grace glances up from the sidewalk and then back down, so quickly and so blankly that I don't really know if she told her Mom I tried to steal it (which I did not) or if I was doing a good deed (which I was but not the way most people would have done it).

Without saying anything else, Trisha James turns and walks the opposite direction, and Grace follows her.

Mom frowns at me. "Do I even want to know?"

I shake my head, and we catch up with Dad and Enzo. But it leaves me to wonder: What would I ever be able to do for that answer to be *yes?*

4

The next day, Enzo and I walk to the university with bags from the cafe next door, each containing a slice of cake with a lemony glaze. I carry mine with the perfectly crisp fold between my fingers so I can have the satisfaction of uncurling the paper just before breakfast. It seems to me like something Grace would do—something precise and orderly. I wonder, briefly, if I'll see her today. Language camp doesn't start until tomorrow, so she may not be planning to hang out with me and Enzo while our parents sit through their meeting.

I may have only met her once so far, but I'm fairly certain Grace would not have reacted the way I did in front of the counter when Mom told us she was buying us a slide of traditional "everyday" Italian cake.

"*Everyday* cake? For breakfast?" I asked too loudly in the cafe while several people turned their heads to look at us. I pumped my fist up to the painted tin ceiling. "That's what I'm talking about!"

"Be cool, Mia," says Enzo, but I can tell by the light in his eyes that he's just as intrigued as I am by these people who eat everyday cake for breakfast. Every day!

"It's not like birthday cake, Mia, so calm down. And most people don't actually have it every day. It'll still be a treat for us; they'll have food for you at language camp tomorrow. And I'm pretty sure it won't be cake."

Mom and Dad find their badges and check in, and Dad helps usher us down a hallway. There's a large glass window that's just slightly shaded, and I do a double take as I pass. It looks like a little nursery with napping babies wrapped in blankets and tiny toddlers making wobbly steps across the foam floor.

"Woah, baby central," I say.

Enzo looks too, and we both laugh when a little girl reaches with all of her might to knock over a block tower, falls along with it, and lands on her diapered bottom.

"In Italy, more workplaces have daycares," says Mom. "Not like in the US, where employers find it more convenient to just pretend their employees don't have the burden of raising children."

Burden.

It hits me right in the stomach. Dad agrees lightly, and they walk on, expecting us to follow. I do, though my legs feel a little heavier.

"Come on, Mia," says Enzo, but I can tell by his tone that he heard it too. "At least we don't have class today. And there's still cake for breakfast."

I do my best to shrug it off and pretend it doesn't bother me as we all walk into an empty lounge. It's got a large carpet spread across the floor with mismatched furniture and books crammed onto the shelves, just like the department lounges back home. Dad teaches math, and Mom teaches economics, which sound like the same thing but aren't, although I don't really know the difference. When I say they both teach math, mom gets mad, and when I say they both teach economics, she gets madder. But their offices are in the same building, meaning Enzo and I have spent a lot of time in rooms like this one.

"See you at lunch," Dad says, winking.

"When is that?" Enzo asks.

"Well," he scratches his head, "the agenda says we'll have a lunch break at noon, but you have to understand that this isn't like the USA. Schedules are a little looser around here. It might be noon, or it might be two, or any time before or after that. But we will have a break for lunch. I think."

"You think?" asks Enzo again. I'm concerned too—this cake feels heavy, but I'm going to get hungry again before two.

"Don't worry. Think of it as immersion."

"What's immersion?" I ask.

"Immersion is letting go of the familiar and just fully diving into something new. Not standing in front of something unfamiliar with one foot in and one foot back. Standing with both feet rooted in your new life."

Enzo rolls his eyes. "Our father, the poet."

Dad does an elaborate bow as a joke and then reaches his arms out to hug me. I squeeze him tighter than he does.

"I'll immersion, Dad," I say.

"You'll *immerse* yourself," he says, I guess as a way of correcting me, but I like that phrase, too—I'd much rather do something for myself than to just do something.

"Keep an eye on her, Enzo," says Dad, but Enzo's already got his headphones in and is draping his legs over the arm of the coziest-looking chair in the room.

"Excuse me," says a voice behind Dad. Grace is in the hallway all by herself.

"You kids have fun," Dad says and goes off to join the other faculty.

"Hi," I say to Grace, but she doesn't answer. She doesn't even look at me; she just walks straight to the armchair across from Enzo and pulls out a book.

"Hey," I say before she can start reading, "thanks for not telling your mom that I stole her purse."

She glares at me over the rims of her oversized cateye glasses. They'd be cute if they were a different color—red would be cute, or maybe even purple. But they're tortoiseshell, which means she doesn't look cute in them at all. She looks sophisticated. "Who says I didn't tell her that?"

"Well, the police didn't come back to our apartment, so I figured you just told her that I'd found it."

"As a matter of fact," she says, crossing her legs to sit criss-cross applesauce in her chair. "I *did* tell her you stole it, but she didn't believe me. She told me you were probably just going to return it after you went to the bathroom."

"That's what I *was* going to do," I say, even as her frown deepens, and her eyes go into her book but do not move. "I just—"

"I'm *reading.*"

She's not reading, because behind those tortoise-shell frames, her eyes stay still on one spot on the page. But I don't need her to tell me I'm wrong again, so I sigh and take out my breakfast. I look out the window while I eat the cake. Judging by the shape, I thought it might taste like an angel food cake, flavorless and spongy, but to my delight, it's not at all like that—it's rich, soft, and fruity. The texture is heavy, filling, but the lemon flavor is light, and two bites in, I decide it's the most delicious thing I've ever eaten. I let it take all of my attention. Only after most of it is gone and I chase after the crumbs at the bottom of the bag do I begin to watch the people moving outside on the street and play one of my favorite alone games—making up stories about the people I see. *That lady was the daughter of a Duke before she met a roofer, and they fell in love and moved to Rome. That man makes the best ravioli on the block, but that other man's life's ambition is to beat him at his own game. That man just stole a necklace, and that's why he's trying to get away fast.* I'd love to get my hands on one of those little scooters the man zips away on—Dad says they're called mopeds—and explore the city. I daydream about it while I lick the glaze from my fingers. I check the loose tooth, but it hasn't budged. I think everyone in my class back home lost their last tooth a long time ago, so I wonder what's going on with this one.

A sound like a growl comes from Grace's stomach. She covers it with her hands.

"Hungry already?" I ask from the windowsill.

"I didn't have breakfast."

I lower my sticky hand. "I'm sorry. I would have shared."

She shakes her head. "It's fine."

But it's not. It's not fair that her mom didn't believe her about me and then didn't get her anything to eat this morning. It's not fair that Grace is already going around with a sour expression on her face when she just arrived in Rome for the summer. She goes back to her book, her shoulders drooping inward lower than they were before, and the sight of her wilting before my eyes is more than I can bear.

I turn my gaze back to the window. Well, she's bitter about me and her mom, but it's not like we're ganging up against her. It's no reason to be rude. She should get over it.

There's some kind of music down on the street that drifts into my consciousness like a ghost. It takes a few seconds to register, but once I do, I'm completely sure it's the same melody I heard on our first night here, a low waltz, lovely and sad. The need to get outside claws at my focus like a craving, a deep animal instinct—I need to get outside. I do my best to shake it off; I tear my eyes away from the sidewalk below, but the craving persists. I hear myself saying:

"No, that was really good, and you need to taste it. I have some money. I know where the cafe is, and the grownups won't be done for a long time. We'll be there and back quick. Come on, let's go."

Enzo looks up. "Mom and Dad will kill me if you leave."

"So come with us. We can all get another slice."

"I'm not going anywhere."

"Neither am I," says Grace, but she's got a curious light in her eyes. "My therapist says to be careful who your friends are."

"Oh, don't worry, I'm sure you'll be a great friend once you're not hangry anymore."

Before she can respond, I turn to Enzo. "Do you want to come?"

"Negative," he responds, not looking up.

Bummer. But I still move to the door.

"Bye," I say. "Hope Mom and Dad don't find out you let me go and take your phone for the summer."

That's enough to make Enzo look up and scowl. Grace's expression is of mortified shock. I do feel sorry for her, even though I know she doesn't like me. I know what it's like to feel ignored, but her mom seems worse than mine.

I slip outside and take a nice, big breath of the fresh air. There are fragrant purple flowers planted in giant clay pots on either side of the door, but instead of lingering longer to smell them like I want to, I move on and get some distance between me and the university. The scents of the street—fumes from the delivery trucks, coffee from the tables on the sidewalks, perfumes from little boutiques—they all smell like adventure to me, though I do wish someone was here to share it with me.

An iron archway looks like it might be the entrance to a park, and I'm about to go check it out when one of the bottom corners of the archway squiggles and curls a little. I squint and realize it's a black cat against the black iron. When it turns it head to look at me, I realize it's not just any cat, it's my friend from the fire escape.

The cat crosses the sidewalk and starts to go out into the traffic on the street. Instantly my heart jumps. As soon as I see the cat step into the street, I know that's the reason I just had to get out here—it's up to me to save him.

I have to act fast. I dart toward the street and call to him: "Here, kitty kitty!" He looks at me innocently and walks beside the sidewalk, on the road. There are parked scooters and cars there, but what if one doesn't see him and pulls out? I can't let him get hurt.

On the streets, I am only vaguely aware that other people and their babies and their little shopping carts are in my way. Some of them move aside for me and give me frustrated or frightened looks, but I don't care. I need to get this cat someplace safe. He moves fluidly into an alley, but I'm still worried he's going to get himself hurt, so I follow. Now I'm only catching glimpses here and there—a tail, a leg, a flash of black as he jumps across a puddle.

I'm so close that I'm nearly crying, and I don't know why. There's a part of me that realizes this is crazy, but I just don't care. Stopping, at this point, feels impossible, like my body is moving all by itself, and I'm powerless to stop it.

Finally, I hear his soft *grrowl* and follow it.

He meows again, louder, again and again, until other sounds join. A tinkling bell, a soft snare, and something else, warm and low—a clarinet, maybe?—accompany the man singing. It sounds so beautiful that I feel like I can no longer stand it. I start to run toward it down a narrow alley with big, silver stones on either side of me. I reach out both of my hands and skim the stones with my fingertips while I run.

The alley opens into a square. When I get to the end, I freeze in amazement.

A chilly wind blows just in front of my face, and brightly-colored bunting ripples overhead in the crisp breeze. The slow waltz floats by on the air as a crowd of children walk around, playing games, talking, laughing, and watching performers. There's a couple of jugglers tossing and catching rings and pins, which spin in front of them in a kaleidoscope of color. A girl in a sparkly white leotard and tights does slow, controlled handstands, her palms pressing on the ground while she makes graceful shapes with her legs in the air. And, in the center, a cluster of kids point and laugh at two puppets dancing to accordion music on a colorful stage.

When I step into the square, the cold air embraces me, and it seems that I've found myself in a different season all together: no longer the beginning of summer, but the end of autumn. It's a welcome change; I hadn't realized I'd been sweating trying to find the cat.

Something warm and furry rubs against my leg.

"There you are," I whisper, and pick him up. He settles down like a baby in my arms. "Well, you found something worth exploring, didn't you?"

I walk around with the content cat purring against my heart. I'm drawn to the puppets who stop their dancing and begin having some kind of an argument. I can't understand what they're saying, but the falsetto tone becomes increasingly shrill and angry. Their voices have a little variation, but not much—one is high-pitched and the other one is higher-pitched. One has a little club in its hands. The first one turns away for a moment, and the second hits him with the club. The first falls to the edge of the stage. Instead of backing up, the one with the club hits him again, and again, until the little pointed hat falls off. But the one with the club keeps going. He hits his fellow puppet until the sound of wood on wood reverberates through the square. The children laugh and laugh. Whoever was controlling the puppet has taken their hand away so that the fallen puppet is lying there lifeless and limp. The second puppet keeps hitting it. Some of its hair flies off. The sound of the children's laughter echos, haunting and cruel.

It makes me feel uneasy in my stomach in a way I don't quite understand. It's just a toy—just fabric and wood and paint—but now I want to leave. I take a step back and bump into something. That something's stomach growls.

"Grace!" I say, more surprised than I mean to. She looks strange here in this square. A gust of wind blows through the alley and flings her hair upward and does the same to a pile of dead leaves behind her until she looks like a conjurer. She looks maybe just as surprised to see me, though—in fact, she's looking at me like the cat and I have switched heads or something. "What?"

"I thought you were going to go to the bakery," she said.

"I was, but then..." I look down at the cat, whose happy purring has stopped. He's glaring at Grace.

She wrinkles her nose. "Is that a stray? He probably has fleas, you know."

37

"He's my friend. He came to my window on our first night."

"Probably not the same cat."

I frown. "He definitely is. See his chest? See his paw?"

I reach down to show her, but when my hand makes contact with his white toe, he jumps down, hisses at us both, and runs toward a boy about our age. The boy picks him up, like he's his pet, and carries him into a tent.

"See?" says Grace. "It looks like he belongs to that boy."

That is what it looks like, I have to admit. "I guess," I say, like I'm not hurt by this. I know Mom and Dad wouldn't let me keep him, but I had already begun to think of him as mine. "He needs to do a better job at taking care of his cat, though. He almost got run over." I turn to her, putting on a who-cares air. "Well, what should we do first?"

"Do?" she says, squinting her eyes at me.

I put the puppet show out of my mind and look around the square. Someone's selling some kind of baked goods in a little cart. I grab her hand, which is freezing cold.

She says, "We should go back," at the same time I say, "Let's get some cannoli!"

I can tell her heart's not in it as much as mine is, and I've got her hand, so I pull her into the square, and she doesn't struggle. The man selling the cannoli smiles at me. "I've never seen you before," he says in English. "Is this your first time at the *Carnivale de Osso?*"

Grace bristles, but I just dig in my backpack for some cash. "Uh-huh. Can we have two, please?"

His unchanging smile goes from me to Grace to the cannoli, which he puts into two crinkly red-and-white striped paper bags and hands to us. "No charge," he says. "We're just glad you're here. Walk around. See what you like best."

"Wow, thanks!" I say. I can feel the man's eyes following us, and I can feel the hesitation in Grace's movements, and I kind of wish both of them would just stop it. This is exactly the kind of thing I hoped to stumble upon in Rome—something exciting, finally. Grace and I walk to a bench and sit. "Have you ever had cannoli?"

She's looking at the pastry as if it might bite her. "I'm not sure if we should eat this."

"What? No, it's delicious." I chomp into it. The doughy outer layer is still warm and crispy, but not too sweet, letting the cream inside take center stage. The chocolate chips, sprinkled on top, are much better than the ones back home. They're not waxy at all, but smooth, rich, and just at the right stage of melted. "Mmm, please eat it. I cannot go through this experience alone, you just have to try."

She takes a bite, and then another, and we do not talk until both are gone. I'm dragging my finger across the paper bag to get some more crumbs and cream when she says:

"I thought they might be poison, the way he was looking at us."

I snort. "He was just being nice. You know? Nice? Ever heard of it?"

Her features harden again. "I'm very nice to people who deserve it."

"I got you a cannoli. Does that count? Am I deserving now?"

She sighs. "Sorry. My therapist says I need to be more open and trust people more. So yeah, thank you for that. But let's go back now."

"What? No way! We just got here! And you heard the cannoli man—we should walk around."

"My mom'll be mad if I'm not there when she gets back."

"Okay, but what's the earliest they could possibly break for lunch?" I ask, balling up the paper bag and tossing it into a trash can. It flies right inside, the middle of the bullseye, a perfect shot. That seems like a good sign—if she thinks I'm cool, she'll stick around. "Noon? It's not even ten yet. We could hang out here for another hour and a half and have plenty of time to get back to the classroom they stuffed us in. Are you really going to come all the way to Rome and then spend all of your time in whatever prison your mom locks you in? What about what you want?"

She doesn't answer, so I stand and sling my backpack on again. "There's a band setting up over there. Let's go listen."

There are quilts laid out on the cobblestone plaza for people to sit on while they watch. A boy waves us over and gestures for us to sit next to him on a yellow one. We do.

"Thanks," I whisper.

He looks like he wants to say something: he even opens his mouth, but no words come out.

"I'm sorry, I only speak English," I tell him.

He looks kind of familiar, and I try to think of where I've seen him before, but the music starts and right away, it's so beautiful that I let myself go into a trance, just feeling it in my bones. I let the cold wind whip my hair and lean slightly closer to Grace. The songs aren't like the ones back home—one bleeds into another, so there's no break, no resolution, no clapping. The music changes every now and then from something fun and bouncy to something else, slow and thoughtful, and then back again.

"Mia," Grace says in a low voice.

It's like being jolted awake again. "Mmmhm?" I manage.

"Do you notice that everyone here..." She licks her lips and looks around. "Is a kid?"

I look. And she's right. All around us, the crowds of people are short, smiling, shrieking kids. The oldest here can't be more than thirteen or fourteen years old, and the youngest four or five. It's kind of like school if there were no teachers. There are no babies, no adults, no older teenagers, no old people.

"But..." I sputter, looking around, looking into young face after young face, "the cannoli man..."

"All of the performers are grown-ups," she says, quiet and sure of herself. "Everyone who looks like they work for the carnival is. And they all have the same face. But the only people here watching them are kids. Doesn't that seem odd to you? And did you hear what that man called this place? *Carnivale de Osso*."

"What does that mean?"

"*Bone Carnival*."

"How do you know that?"

"I'm not as bad at Italian as my mom thinks I am. But don't you think this is all a little weird?"

The truth is that it does make my gut feel a little queasy. But maybe that's just the combination of cake and pastry for breakfast. I hope that's the reason, anyway.

"No," I say, mustering confidence. I've learned that people will trust almost anything you say if you say it confidently. "Bone is probably just someone's name, like how we have Barnum and Bailey circuses. And it's probably just a carnival for kids. Italian parents are just more laid-back than American ones."

"Really?" She raises her eyebrows in surprise, but she seems to want to believe me almost as much as I want to believe myself.

I have no idea. "Really! They probably just let the kids come here by themselves. We're lucky we snuck out; it would have been so embarrassing to be here with one of our moms."

"Oh," she says, re-crossing her legs underneath her. "Okay then. Let's just stay for this magic show, then."

A man steps out onto the stage and begins setting up a small wooden table with his back to us. He's tall, thin, and mustached, wearing all black except for a blood-red ribbon that ties his hair into a ponytail at the nape of his neck. As soon as he appears, the band starts another song, that same slow melody, and without thinking about it, I hum along.

"Okay, I really think we should go." Grace grabs my hand and tries to pull me up.

"What?" I jerk my hand back. "No. Why?"

"I didn't know how to tell you this, but you were acting really weird. I thought it might be, like, normal for you, but I didn't know you thought you were following someone. You were basically wandering aimlessly on the sidewalk, you went back and forth a few times. You were singing."

"What? No, I was following that cat. I was trying to call it, but I wasn't singing."

"No, Mia." Her face is stone. "You were. You were singing."

I roll my eyes. "Did it sound like, *here, kitty kitty.*"

"No. You were singing this song."

I stop humming and slowly become aware that all the other kids in the crowd are softly singing the words to this song, as if it's a theme song we're all meant to know. *You were singing this song,* she'd said. Was I?

Now it feels like there are snakes in my stomach slithering in different directions under my hot skin. The man onstage is taking something out of a hard black case. "I don't know what you're talking about, but I'm not going back right now. Go back if you want, but you can't tell me what to do. You're not my mom."

Her eyes are a mix of fear and disbelief, but just then, several more carnival workers pull a massive sheet of dark purple fabric above our heads and fasten it to stakes in the ground behind us, making a tent around us. She stands but doesn't go, and I can't tell whether she thinks she's protecting me or if she's too afraid to go back by herself. If she needs someone to take her back, then fine, I will—but not until I feel like going back.

"Welcome, children." The man swishes his cape and steps forward, his black boots making a hollow *thump* on the stage. He's speaking in English for some reason, which I'm grateful for. "Welcome to the main event of the *Carnival de Osso*. Please take your seats; the show is about to begin."

"Don't you want to stay and find out what this show is all about?" I whisper. "If we leave now, we'll never know."

Grace seems to be the kind of person who waits for other people to tell her what to do, which is fine by me. Almost everyone back in Louisville is like that, and it just meant that I was the one who got to make most of the decisions. "Fine," she mumbles.

More sheets of silk are pulled around the sides of the tent, and the kids around us *ooh* and *ahh* over the rippling purple walls of the tent. Now we're completely enclosed. Someone shines a spotlight on the man, who smiles and steps aside. Another puppet, a marionette on long strings, is lowered down beside him. It's obviously meant to look like him, with the same long nose, the same narrow waist, the same dark ponytail. The same face as the cannoli man—I can see it now. The puppet walks with amazingly lifelike movements toward us, brings a palm to his mouth, and blows. I swear I can see it breathe in and out. A purple fog grows from his hand and fills the inside of the tent.

"Amazing effects!" I whisper, almost to myself. I've never seen a puppet do that before.

When the fog clears, there are two puppets on the stage—a young boy and a woman, who I guess is supposed to be his mom. They act out the story and the man narrates.

"Long ago, Gozzelino was a child born into a family of sorcerers. Like his mother and his grandfather and his grandfather's father before him, the little boy was born with a fantastic magic in his bones. Magic to make them rich, powerful, and lucky beyond imagination. Anything the family wanted, even a little, was theirs with little or no effort.

Little Gozzelino loved his mother. She taught him how to use his magic to get anything he wanted, and they enjoyed their charmed life until a powerful illness came to Rome."

Here, from one side of the stage, the narrator pauses and waves a hand. Streams of black fog waft from under the tent's walls, straight toward the two marionettes. As before, the tent is suddenly filled with the dark cloud, making my heart skip a beat, but it dissipates almost as soon as it starts. When the air is clear again, only the little boy puppet remains onstage.

"The plague took tens of thousands of lives, including Gozzelino's family. His mother's magic could not save them from death. It made Gozzelino angry, and then determined."

The puppet takes a doll-sized knife and cuts off one of his wooden fingers. It falls to the floor, but he picks it up and holds it up high. A caldron is lowered onto the stage, and little Gozzelino places the finger inside. Beside me, Grace squirms, but I am intrigued. This little play is weird, yes, but maybe this is what Dad meant about immersing myself in a new culture. Some things are bound to seem odd in a new country, right?

"Gozzelino used one of his own magic bones to create what would be his greatest achievement: an elixir that could cure all disease. No one on earth would have to die again the way his mother died. No longer would he be lazy and use his magic only to enrich himself, as his family had done for generations. Gozzelino worked for the next ten years with focus and discipline. But the plague never completely left. When he had grown into a young man, sickness came next for him.

"The elixir wasn't finished. He needed more time. It wasn't fair that he had spent his life, his time, his magic on a cure for something that just bided its time to claim his life as well. As he grew sicker and closer to death in his bed, a carnival outside his window seemed to mock his pain with its bright colors and lively music."

The puppet gets out of bed and walks toward the end of the stage, toward us. Without thinking, I lean back.

One day, when he could stand it no longer, Gozzelino threw open his window to curse the carnival. Until that day, he had never attempted to use his magic to curse anyone, and the curse turned out to be more powerful than he'd intended. The carnival and everyone inside was entirely at his service. Gozzelino realized then that it could be put to use. And that is the story of how the *Carnivale de Osso* began."

The narrator claps his hands twice. The unseen puppeteer lifts Gozzelino up and away.

"Wait," I whisper to Grace. "Did I miss something? What did the curse do? What use did he have for the carnival?"

She makes a sound that's something between a squeak and a hiccup. It's only then I see how terrified she looks.

"Your attendance here today helps the ongoing work of perfecting the magic elixir and curing all disease around the world. To convey my thanks, I will now choose one of you for a special honor."

From his pocket, he pulls a midnight-blue velvet pouch, the same size as his palm. I can only guess what's supposed to be inside. I lean forward.

"In this bag is Gozzelino's magic bone. Today we will choose the next keeper, who will be lucky in whatever they attempt as long as the sun shines today."

It's definitely a weird story but also cool and creepy. I like how cannoli guy is dressed up like Gozzelino—it makes it a little spookier. Poor Grace, though: I kind of like being scared for fun like this, but I guess it's not her thing.

"Grace—are you okay? You look like you're going to barf."

She nods silently, and I have an urge to reach out and put my arm around her. I don't know how she'd react to that, though—we've already had a rocky start, and I am glad she's here with me, so I don't want her to stop talking to me because I've done something stupid. Then I have an idea: if there's a chance that bone really is lucky, then maybe we could have an adventure together for the rest of the day. She and I could run around Rome all day without getting caught, and maybe I'd have a real friend while I'm here. She's probably going to say it's dumb, but it's worth a shot, anyway. I need someone to be a bad influence on if I'm going to spend this summer doing something other than conjugating Italian verbs and translating sentences.

The narrator sweeps his cape back with an elegant flourish. "Do I have any brave volunteers?"

My hand shoots into the air out of pure habit—I always volunteer.

But mine is the only one raised. The crowd turns and looks at me, fear written on every face.

5

"Mia," Grace hisses into my ear. "Put your hand down."

But the man has already seen me, and his lips curl into a smile as he beckons me beside him onstage.

Suddenly I'm not feeling brave at all. Does everyone know something I don't? I wish I had thought for a second before I'd raised my hand, and I wish I hadn't judged Grace so harshly for her suspicion and hesitation. Nevertheless, I gulp and make my way slowly through the crowd of kids, like I'm wading through freezing water.

When I get to the shadow man, he reaches out his arm to me. Though he's wearing gloves, I shudder when his icy cold hand lands on my shoulder.

"The first volunteer. Excellent. Does anyone wish to challenge her for this honor?"

I realize, too late as always, I have no idea what I've volunteered for. The crowd of children stays quiet, their hands in their laps, their elbows squeezed into their sides so there's no doubt about their lack of desire to stand beside me. And now that I have a good view of their faces, I notice something strange: they don't look like they just came off the street, like me and Grace. They're dressed in old-fashioned clothes, like they're all in costume for some kind of play, but from different times. And even stranger than that, their color is off. Even in this low light, their faces have a grayish-purple cast that makes them look almost dead. I wonder why I didn't see this before. Did I just not look closely enough? Did Grace notice it?

I glance at Grace, who definitely stands out in the crowd. Amid all these dull faces, she almost glows. But she's scared, more so than before, and her expression stirs something inside me. She was right: something is off, and we need to go. I take a baby step back.

"You know, actually..." My insides are boiling. "I changed my mind. I'd rather just watch."

He snatches my wrist. The leather of his gloves are so well-worn they feel sort of like loose, soft skin, and I can feel the chill of his fingers through them. "Oh, no. You are my brave volunteer, and today you are awarded for your bravery. There is no need to compete, since the rest of your fellow spectators are content to remain just that. Like many great leaders before you, you have proved your worthiness simply by raising your hand." He lets go of my wrist and draws out a long, golden cord from the blue pouch. He lowers it around my neck like a necklace. It feels like nothing, but I shudder when I remember it supposedly contains a dead man's finger.

Now he grips my shoulders and looks into my eyes. His are pale blue, contrasting starkly with his thick, dark eyelashes. "You'll have a lifetime's worth of luck today, my dear. Use it well."

I gulp and nod. "Thanks. And...do I bring this back tomorrow?"

"I will get it back; do not worry about that."

I don't like the sound of that, but I don't have any time to react. The walls and ceiling of the tent are being rolled away by the familiar-looking carnival workers, costumed in harlequin-patterned leotards and tights. The kids in front of me all get up from their places on the ground and run in all directions. Only Grace stays still, staring at me and giving me a look as though I've just been summoned to the principal's office.

"Now run along," shadow man says. "Enjoy the carnival."

"Thanks, uh—"

"Gozzelino," he says, sweeping down into a low bow. "At your service."

Until literally seconds ago, all of this seemed like a big show—he and the Gozzelino puppet were dressed alike for the act. But the way he says the name sounds different. It doesn't sound like an actor saying his stage name. It sounds like he's said it many, many times before. It sounds like his name. And for the first time, I am truly afraid.

I give Grace a look that says *let's get out of here* and she shoots me another one that says *finally*. We walk shoulder-to-shoulder towards the alley with our eyes to the ground until we're out on the main street again, among the familiar sights of street signs, the sounds of hissing busses, and scents of car exhaust lingering in the air. Best of all, the temperature is warmer, and thicker, and the air on my skin feels like the safety of being under a weighted blanket. Both of us breathe a sigh of relief.

"That was weird," I say.

"You're telling me," she says. "At first I thought it was a carnival for like, sick kids, usually in the hospital or something. But then I noticed every grown-up looked like that Gozzelino guy, and I knew something had to be off."

"Maybe they were all in one family."

"Maybe."

"Maybe all those kids were sick."

"Yeah, I guess they could've been. None of them were talking much."

"Then again," I say, pulling the pouch out of the front of my shirt, "Maybe this really is lucky after all."

Grace's eyes widen. "I think we should put that back."

I ignore her and feel the pouch from the outside. Now that we're not at the carnival anymore, it feels much safer, and I'm already wondering why I was so freaked out. From the outside of the soft, worn velvet, I can feel a long and fragile-feeling object. "Eww!" I shriek and giggle a little. "I think there really is a finger in here!"

"Let's just go drop it back off. We'll be quick."

"Or," I say, raising one eyebrow at her and leaning in, "we could test our luck. We could eat gelato, see the Parthenon, go to the Vatican and sneak behind the velvet ropes..."

"Stop it!" she says, stomping her foot on the sidewalk. "You don't know what my mom would do to me if she knew I was out here, not to mention any of that!"

I sigh. As much as I want to tell her that her mom can't legally kill her, I can play the long game if it means we can be friends soon. "Okay, fine. We'll go back and drop this bone off with the carnie creepsters, and then we'll go back."

She looks suspicious, but nods. "Promise?"

"Promise," I say, "But I think we should stop and get gelato on the way back."

"Mia," she says in a grumpy tone.

"Only if we see a place on the way."

"Fine," she says. "Okay, well...let's go."

I nod at her, and we turn back toward the alley. Immediately, the squirming sensation comes back to me, but not for the same reasons as before. Before, it felt like a warning, a premonition, a way my body tried to tell me to get out of there...now the feeling is more like dread.

Because now, there is no music. We can see the square through the alley, and as we walk closer, I can see that it's all different. The cold wind is gone. The tents are gone. The performers and the children and the puppets are gone.

There are some bistro tables set up with some adults having coffee at them and waiters weaving through the tables with pads of papers in their hands. A teenage couple sits on one side of the fountain, holding hands. A man walks out of one of the cafes and throws a bag of trash into a dumpster.

"What the..." I mutter, but truly it's hard to describe the feeling. It's like I can't believe what I'm seeing right in front of me.

"Oh, Mia," whispers Grace. "I think this is bad."

My eyes linger on the dumpster. "Let's throw the bone in there and go back to the university," I say.

She nods vigorously and silently but makes no other movement. I realize I'm the one who actually has to do it as the bone is around my neck. I take it off, gripping the cord in my fist. I feel to make sure the bone really is in the pouch, and this time, when I feel the hard object inside, I shudder.

Just do it, I tell myself. I make my way to the dumpster, hold my breath, open the lid, and toss the velvet pouch inside.

Walking away, I do feel better, and somehow lighter. I smile at Grace, who actually smiles back.

"Now let's go," she says.

We make our way back and though I don't really know where I'm going, she seems to know, so I follow her. After a while, though, she asks, "Do you know which way we go now?"

"No," I say. "I thought you knew."

She huffs. "I told you. You were going all kinds of weird ways, singing to yourself and wandering around."

I groan. "You're just going to have to ask someone."

"Me? Why don't you do it?"

"Because you're the one who speaks Italian."

She looks uncomfortable but eventually she does approach an elderly woman waiting for a bus. They speak a few words to each other, and the woman points a gnarled finger in the direction we were already going.

Not even two blocks later, we're there. Just around a corner, the clock tower looms and strikes eleven. Both of us breathe a sigh of relief.

"Thanks for asking that lady," I say.

"No problem," she says, brightening. "I actually feel pretty proud of myself. I've only ever spoken Italian to my tutor; I've never actually talked to anyone in another language for real."

"You did great," I say.

She grins and looks up at the clock tower. "My therapist sometimes tells me I have to do hard things to prove to myself that I can."

I don't really understand that, but I let it go. I don't want to make her all jumpy again by asking too many questions. "Well, it's just too bad we didn't find anywhere to buy—"

"Gelato!" Someone yells from somewhere on our right side. "Gelato!"

There's a little stand here on the street—a white cart with a matching umbrella and a young man dressed in a yellow-and-white striped apron. He's looking at us and smiling.

Grace and I look at each other, and then go toward the cart. He says something as we approach.

"He says they only have lemon today."

"That's my favorite!" I say. It's true. I would have chosen lemon out of a hundred flavors.

"It is?" asks Grace. "That's my favorite too!"

We laugh and pay for the gelato. I'm glad that he actually takes our money, unlike cannoli man. And then I remember that I'd like to forget about the cannoli man, and the entire carnival.

We take our cups to a bench in front of the clock tower and sit in the cool, shady grass under a giant oak tree. It feels almost too perfect, like I'm having a real adventure, only better than I imagined, because Grace is here, and she's not mad at me anymore. In fact, it feels like we really went through something together, and we could actually be real friends, not just friendly because we're the same age and in the same place. She leans down to tuck her lace back into her shoe, and I catch a whiff of her hair. It smells like peppermint.

"I was thinking of that movie you mentioned—*Roman Holiday*, right?" asks Grace, sitting back up.

"I thought you said you'd never heard of it."

"I haven't, but I think it's cool that you like old movies like that. Maybe on Saturday you could come over and we could watch it."

I almost choke on my gelato. "Really?"

She nods. "I mean, if my mom says it's okay. I was nervous about starting language camp, but asking that lady for directions made me realize I'm actually not bad. So if I bring home some sort of good report from the first week, I have a feeling she'll be okay with it."

"Yeah," I say, "That'd be great. I guess good grades are really important to your mom, huh?"

She brings a leaf close to her knee and traces its veins with her finger. "Yeah. My therapist says it has nothing to do with me. She has a sister, my aunt, and she has a daughter, my cousin. I don't know what happened between my mom and my aunt, but they have this weird competition going between us. If my cousin Nicole wins a karate competition or sells the most Girl Scout cookies in her troupe or something, my mom's mad at me for a week. And if I make the honors roll, which I always do, she calls my aunt first, before she even congratulates *me*."

"Geez," I say. "What does your dad say about it?"

"My dad left when my mom was pregnant with me. He lives in Arizona with his new family. I usually go to visit him for a week in the spring and fall, but I don't think he's very interested in me. And I'd feel weird telling him about Mom and my aunt."

"Is this why you talk to your therapist so much?"

She suddenly looks really unhappy. "Yeah."

I stare down into my gelato, letting myself just feel her sadness for a few seconds.

"Well," I say slowly, "Your cousin isn't here. The only person she has to compare you to now is me, which is awesome for you. My Italian is awful."

Grace smiles. "This summer is the first time ever it's just me and Mom. I think if I just do well at this language camp thing, it could really change things. She could finally be actually proud of me, and then maybe she won't care what my aunt thinks."

"It's cool that you even know what your mom's deal is. My parents are not proud of me either, but they usually just get mad and then get over it pretty fast. It's like they get tired of caring."

"Why do you think they're not proud of you?"

"I don't know. I do things without thinking first. I can't help it."

"Can you really not help it?" asks Grace.

I lick my lips and look around, letting my eyes rest on a bird taking a bath in a puddle. "I don't think so. I mean, usually it's not a problem, because they're not around, and I can just do whatever I feel like doing. They're always busy."

"I know what that feels like," says Grace. But somehow I feel like she's just saying that to make me feel better. If her mom is as obsessed with her good grades as she says she is, there's no way she can understand how my parents ignore me most of the time, how Enzo and I sometimes spend entire weekends in front of the TV because my parents are working, how they'll sign us up for every camp and sport and activity and after-school program just so they don't have to spend time with us, except when they want to. And how when we do hang out as a family, they always, always post it on Facebook, and it makes it feel like that's the only reason they're spending any time with us. I think about telling her all of this, but I say nothing. It's probably normal, for the most part.

The wet bird flies away.

"Can you believe that there was a gelato cart right there?" asks Grace. "And he only had our favorite flavor?"

"Lucky us," I say, and as soon as I say the word, both of us freeze, with our spoons halfway raised to our mouths.

"Mia," she says slowly, lowering her spoon down into her cup, "You did put that...that thing in the dumpster, right?"

My fingers fumble in front of my heart, I reach into the front of my shirt, and, sure enough, I pull out the pouch, still somehow strung around my neck.

6

My stomach drops, and the ground sways under my feet. I'm suddenly a mixture of sickness and confusion—How is this possible?

Grace's eyes are saucers. "I thought you threw that away."

"I did," I say. "I know I did."

But did I? Here it is, after all, the cord still around my neck and the pouch in my hands. Did I just imagine I threw it away?

"We have to get rid of it, for real this time," she says, as if that's not the most obvious thing that's ever been said out loud. I'm about to ask how she suggests doing that when a group of adults pour out of the university's doors.

"Oh no," I say, and we sprint back up to the room where we were supposed to stay put for the past four hours.

We fly up the staircase, past the plaques and portraits of stern-faced professors from years past. From the door to the second floor, I arrive just in time to see my dad walk inside the room.

"Where are they, then?" my mom asks

Beside me, Grace trembles, but I'm an old pro at this. "Where are who?" I ask in my most innocent voice. Mom turns around.

"Oh, there you are," says Mom. "Ready to go to lunch?"

"Sure," I say. "Where's Grace's mom?"

"Dr. James asked us if we'd mind bringing you to the dining hall. She had a question for one of the administrators, but she'll meet us there."

"Sounds great," I say, and the five of us walk down the hall as if nothing at all had happened, even as the bone in the velvet pouch thumps against my heart.

We're slowed on the steps by a large crowd gathered in the hallway. People are mumbling in all different languages, but it's hard to know what's going on. I climb a few steps and look out over everyone's heads just in time to see a lady come out of what must be the dining hall. A smoky stream escapes with her. She says something in Italian, and almost everyone in the crowd walks outside via the large glass doors on our right.

"What'd she say?" I ask nobody in particular.

"There was a minor fire in the dining hall, and they want us all to go outside," answers Mom. She narrows her eyes at me. "Mia, tell me you didn't—"

"I was with Grace the whole time!" I've had lots of practice saying non-lies, but I'm not even sure it's necessary here. I think I'd remember setting a fire.

"It's true," Enzo says. "She was. And I can't wait any longer. I'm hungry."

"Me too," says Dad. "Look, this is actually lucky. Let's go out to that little cafe we passed this morning. Grace, I'll text your mom, and you can come with us. If we go right now, we may be able to beat the rush."

To my surprise, Mom puts her hand on my back and taps twice. It sends a jolt of joy through my body. Is this seriously happening?

"Okay," says Mom, "let's go."

Twenty minutes later, we're being served soft mozzarella cheese on focaccia bread, drizzled with balsamic vinegar and sprinkled with something green and fragrant.

"Fresh basil," says Dad when he sees me examining it. "You're going to love it."

I'm sure I would love it, but I can't eat anything right now. Everyone else seems too hungry to even notice that Grace and I only pick at our plates.

Dr. James arrives, and Dad gets her a chair. Graces straightens her back and looks at her, but her mom doesn't even acknowledge her. She just hangs her bag on the back of her chair and turns to my mom.

"Apparently the fire was a bit more serious than they thought," she says. "We may not be allowed back inside the building for the rest of the day."

"What about orientation?" asks Mom.

"They say they'll probably send us an email with the rest of the information."

"I had a feeling the entire morning could have been an email," says Dad. "But that's okay. Food tastes better when you're really hungry, anyway. So we're off for the rest of the day today and tomorrow, is that it?"

"That's not all," says Dr. James. "The entire building has to be fumigated. Language camp is off for tomorrow too."

"So we're all off today and tomorrow," says Mom, frowning. "I don't know how I feel about that."

I do.

I feel like my heart is ping-ponging with glee inside my rib cage.

"Well, I'll say it if nobody else will," says Dad, "I'm thrilled. Let's go be tourists for the rest of the day."

"We'll still need to go through that email," says Mom, "Prepare for classes..."

"You know we're ready. As long as they still start next week, we can take a long weekend to relax a little. Let's have some fun!" Finally, he looks at me, probably because he knows I am a dependable member of Team Fun. "Mia, what do you think?"

The bone around my neck feels heavier than it did this morning. I don't know how to get rid of it if tossing it in a giant, smelly dumpster didn't work. "I'm...language camp is really cancelled?"

"Until next week," says Dr. James. "I don't know if Grace can take so much time off from it. It's probably best that we stay in so she can run some drills..."

The waiter sets a glass in front of Dr. James and pours water into it from the oversized glass bottle. Grace suddenly looks at him with a fierceness in her eyes.

"*Mi scusi*," says Grace, and then speaks to him in Italian. He answers a question, and she asks another question. He answers that one, too. Finally, she says "Grazi," and he smiles, takes her glass, refills it, and walks away.

"Sounds like I'm the one who needs language drills," says Enzo. "I wish I could speak Italian like that."

"Your Italian is very good, hon," says Mom, "But he's right, yours is excellent, Grace."

Dr. James is looking at Grace as if seeing her for the first time. "I didn't know you could do that," she says. "You're always forgetting words at home."

Grace picks up her fork and pokes at her caprese again. "It's easier when you switch your brain to thinking in just Italian, not going back and forth between that and English. It feels completely different."

"You need to tutor me," I say, and it's supposed to be a joke, but the corners of Mom's mouth immediately dip as if she's considering it.

"Not a bad idea," she says. "And Grace, that's the power of language immersion. You sort of switch who you are based on what language you're speaking."

"Let's go out today, and we can have the kids do all the talking for us. We'll pretend we only speak English," suggests Dad.

"It's okay with me," says Dr. James, and she puts her palm to Grace's shoulder. Grace beams at her.

Their smiles make me bristle. Now that I know what I do about the weird competition between Dr. James and her sister—and the way they push Grace and her cousin to compete—I don't like that Grace had to prove herself to earn a smile from her Mom.

"Nice!" says Dad. "Here, I was too famished to take a picture of my lunch, but let's post one of all of us here at the table." I can see his thumbs working, but he frowns at his screen.

Inwardly, I sigh. Pics or it didn't happen, I guess.

But Dad doesn't raise his screen. "Huh, that's weird. The Facebook app isn't coming up."

Mom gets hers out and taps the screen. "It's not for me, either. Bad service, I guess."

I still think this bone is probably bad news, but in the meantime, it's gotten us out of that stuffy room, out of language camp, and into a social media-free day with our parents.

"Hey, Mia," says Enzo, glancing at the pouch. "What's that thing?"

I take the velvet in my hands and run my fingers along the soft velvet. Yes, it's creepy. But it's also undeniably lucky, and it might not hurt just to keep it a little longer. "What, this?"

Grace gives me a curious look. I smile at Enzo. "Just a little souvenir. You know, from this morning, when you let me out of the room to—"

"Mom! Dad!" says Enzo suddenly. "Uh...want to talk more about what classes I should be taking next year? I was thinking I might take ceramics in my first year after all!"

Enzo is, undeniably, the master of changing the subject. In seconds, Mom and Dad are talking about the importance of focusing on STEM, and I smile to myself and tuck the pouch into my shirt with the lucky bone still safe inside.

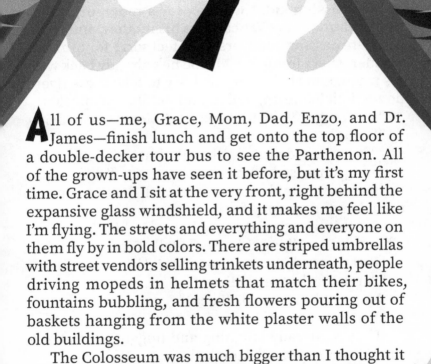

7

All of us—me, Grace, Mom, Dad, Enzo, and Dr. James—finish lunch and get onto the top floor of a double-decker tour bus to see the Parthenon. All of the grown-ups have seen it before, but it's my first time. Grace and I sit at the very front, right behind the expansive glass windshield, and it makes me feel like I'm flying. The streets and everything and everyone on them fly by in bold colors. There are striped umbrellas with street vendors selling trinkets underneath, people driving mopeds in helmets that match their bikes, fountains bubbling, and fresh flowers pouring out of baskets hanging from the white plaster walls of the old buildings.

The Colosseum was much bigger than I thought it would be. I've seen lots of pictures of it—there's even a scene in *Roman Holiday* with it in the background—but it's much bigger than it looks in the movie. And I'm not sure what I expected, but arriving in front of it kind of reminds me of the carnival atmosphere, and that makes me feel a little uneasy, and it makes the bone around my neck feel heavy and noticeable again. We have to park kind of far away, and when we walk up to it, we pass lots of people selling shirts and hats with pictures of swords and shields on them.

I step on something, and my foot slides just a fraction of an inch. I look down and see it's another poster of that missing kid. I wonder, for a moment, if that woman I saw at the Vatican was his mother, and if she was here passing out flyers too. I feel sorry for him and wonder where he's gone. Maybe he's already back with his mom, and she's been too busy to take these flyers down. I pick one up, fold it, and put it in my pocket.

"Don't engage with those people," Mom says suddenly.

"Who?"

"The ones dressed like gladiators," she says, seeming surprised I haven't noticed yet. "They dress up in costumes and take pictures with the tourists and then demand you pay for it."

But this one gladiator guy has us in his sights now. "There's one walking this way," I tell Mom.

"Just pretend you can't understand him," says Mom.

"Sarah?" asks the gladiator.

Mom whirls around. "Luca?"

"You know him?" I ask.

They're already laughing and hugging. "It's been, what? Twenty years?" Mom asks.

"Doesn't seem possible, does it? It's so good to see you! What are you doing here back in Rome?"

Mom tells the gladiator—Luca, I guess—about her new job at the university. Dad comes and puts his hands on my shoulders, waiting, like me, to be introduced.

66

"Luca, this is my husband, Andy, and my daughter, Mia. And my son, Enzo, is over there with some friends of ours."

"The whole family together in the city of love!" he exclaims. "What more could you ask for?"

"I thought Paris was the city of love," I say.

He draws himself up. "Rome is the city of love, and I can prove it. It's right in its name! Reverse the letters of *Roma,* and what do you get? *Amor.*" He opens his arms to us. "Love!"

"Mia, James, this is Luca," Mom says to us. "We're friends from when I spent a year here as a forgeign exchange student in high school."

"Oh, yes," says Dad. "I've heard so much about you."

"All lies!" he says and laughs, just once, like a trumpet blast. And then he leans down to speak to me. "Is this your first time in Rome?"

I nod. He crouches down further, and I find myself hoping he's wearing bike shorts or something under that metal pleated skirt. "I'll tell you a secret: I am not really a Roman gladiator. No, really! I am part of a team that works on the restoration of the Colosseum from time to time, but this costume makes me feel like I am part of history, and it is part of me. I want to feel in my body how they must have felt in theirs two thousand years ago. But the truth is that I know a lot about this building; I'm not here to take pictures with the tourists. Would you like to have a tour?"

"Only if I can try on your helmet," I say, and he laughs again and lifts it from his head. On mine, it feels incredibly heavy, like it's pressing down on my spine.

"Heavier than it looks, huh?" he asks. Enzo and Grace also try it on, and I can see they're also surprised by the weight. "That's what I mean. We're so used to our own clothes that sometimes it helps to understand the people of the past by subjecting our bodies to whatever they subjected theirs to. It's also the reason I don't eat meat! Roman gladiators were called 'bean munchers' and 'barley men' because they mostly ate beans and barley."

"We've mostly eaten desserts all day," I say. I'm just trying to make conversation, but to my surprise, everyone in the group laughs.

"I guess we can't blame you for that," says Luca. "This is a good city for sweets. Now come on, let's go inside. We're very close to the Gate of Life, so we could start there."

"Gate of Life?"

"It's where the gladiators would enter the area. Those men were usually prisoners of war or slaves, but sometimes men would volunteer for the job, even though it was extremely dangerous. They had about a one-in-nine chance of being killed any time they fought to entertain the ancient Romans here. On the other side is where they carried out the unlucky ones, the ones in nine. Can you guess what that is called?"

A shiver goes through my arms, but I can't stop myself from answering anyway. "The Gate of Death?"

"Smart girl," says Luca. "Some say the ghosts of gladiators still linger there to help their brethren to the other side. Come on! I'll show you."

Lines of tourists in sneakers and tank tops snake around the sides of the gigantic building, but Luca flashes a pass at a security guard, and we all walk right past the crowds. Grace quietly pushes her way past her mom and my brother and nudges me in the ribs as we make our way up the cool stone staircase.

"Awfully lucky, isn't it?" she whispers. "We happen to meet a gladiator historian who happens to know your mom who happens to have the time to give us a private tour?"

"Listen," I reply, "I know you think this is a problem, but…can't we just figure it out later? Enjoy the afternoon? See where this takes us?"

"I think we should try to get rid of that bone again."

Grace's earnest eyes are freaking me out. Back at the school, I got the impression she was smart, but how could she be when she actually believes this bone is bringing us luck? It's probably not even a real bone. And I must have just…*thought* that I threw it away.

"Listen. There's no such thing as magic bones."

"No," she jabs a finger at the center of my chest. "*You* listen. There's something wrong with that thing. It's giving me the heebie-jeebies, and it needs to go."

"Okay," I say, drawing out the last syllable. "If it'll make you feel better, sure. If I see a trash can, I'll toss it in."

"You tried that once, remember? It didn't work. I say we listen to the guy in the bean-muncher costume. If we can make it to the Gate of Death, maybe a gladiator ghost can help get Gozzelino's spirit to the other side."

"Wait. You think Gozzelino is…here?"

"A piece of him, anyway. Physically and otherwise. His magic is obviously with us."

I snort. "You really believe in all this?"

"I don't know what I believe anymore!" Her whisper has turned into a hiss. "Just today, I have seen an entire carnival appear and disappear in a few seconds. I saw you throw that creepy bone away, just to have it reappear on your neck a few minutes later. My mom is being nice, my Italian is way better, and now we're in the Colosseum with—" she stops, I think because she notices it at the same time as I do: we've stopped to talk, and our families have gone on with Luca.

We're alone.

In an ancient stone stairwell.

In the Colosseum.

We run up ahead a little, but our families are nowhere to be found. We run around the corner. We run down the hall. We keep running and running, but we don't see our group...or anyone else at all. No tourists. No vendors. And thankfully, no ghosts, though I'm starting to get worried. Who loses everyone—*everyone*—in a place this massive? I start to feel really small, the way I felt when I saw the ocean for the first time. But Grace is still here, and I feel like I can't show her how scared I am.

"Come on," I say. "We'll find them and ask Luca to show us the Gate of Death. If we happen to see any ghosts of any gladiators, we'll ask them to please escort Gozzelino to the other side."

I'm joking, but only kind of. The truth is that I hope Grace is right. As nice as it is to be lucky, I don't want to find out what Gozzelino meant by telling me he'd get the bone back. At this point, I'd prefer to be back looking out a window in a teacher's lounge, like this morning, back when life was boring but safe.

I don't want to be the most interesting person in the room anymore.

"Can you call your mom?" I ask. "I put my phone in my mom's purse."

"I did too," says Grace. "I didn't want to carry it anymore."

I exhale a huff of air. "We'll find them," I say. Come on, let's go down. Luca said the Gate of Death was just on the opposite side. Let's go over there, and then we'll meet them when they come."

We are the only ones to cross the arena. Some groups of tourists dot this entrance or that one among the ruined stone slabs that used to hold seating. Grace catches my hand and pulls me along a side wall. It happens so fast that my breath catches in my throat.

She releases my hand and moves quickly along the wall. There are approximately a million steps between us and the opposite gate, and it's tricky because there are lots of gates between the two as well.

"Grace," I say, "Which one is the Gate of Death?"

She points ahead. "That one? I think? Because we came from..." She spins around and so do I, but I can't see which one we came from. All of the entrances look the same, all circled around the arena. Were the group of tourists in the yellow hats on the right or left side of us? Did we pass them after six entrances or eight?

Her shoulders fall. "We should have paid more attention."

"We'll get there," I say with a tone of determination that I don't exactly feel. "Let's just keep going."

The truth is that I'm starting to feel panicky, like a caged animal. I need to find a way out, and I want to move in fourteen different directions until one works.

We wind around, trying to get to where we think the other side of the arena is. Suddenly, a strange urge comes over me. It's kind of like the urge I felt to jump from my window on our first night in Rome, but now it's unavoidable, unstoppable. I freeze right where I am and put my arm out to stop Grace as well.

I stare straight ahead. I'm not sure what I'm waiting for, but I'm certain this is right—I should go no further. I don't know what it is, only that I should listen to this animal instinct, this warning to go no further. A moment passes. Graces leans forward slightly and says, "Um, Mia? What are—"

And then she stops. Because at that moment, a man steps out of the gate. Although he is dressed like Luca, he looks nothing like him. He wears leather lace-up sandals over his bulging legs and a breastplate over his monstrous chest and shoulders. The way he holds his head tells me he's used to the weight of his helmet. He turns and looks at us, but I cannot look at his face. My eyes, instead, are drawn to his chest, where something enormous has punctured the center, right at his heart. The entire front of his body is stained with blood from the wound.

It takes every bit of willpower to not pee my pants.

He says something.

"Grace?" I whisper, my voice and body shaking with fear, "do you see him too?"

"Yes," she says.

72

He doesn't move, but says the same thing to us again. He's not speaking Italian.

"What is he saying?"

"I...I think it's Latin? But it doesn't sound like the Latin we learned at school," she says. "And I don't know, but I don't think he wants to pose for a picture with us."

I take off the bone necklace, and the ghost's translucent eyes follow my movements.

"Here you go," I say softly. He's not carrying any weapons, but he still looks like he could fling me into the upper stands with his bare hands. "Grace?"

"Yeah?"

"Get ready to run."

"Are you sure that's a good—"

I toss the pouch at the gladiator's leather sandals. "Run!"

We turn and run from behind us, though, to my horror, I can hear more footsteps but no breathing. Giant hands grip both of my shoulders and pull me back. Two gladiators are on either side of me, and another two have Grace. They drag us back to the gate. I close my eyes and grimace. I'm sure we've found it now.

The Gate of Death.

They take us through the gate, and as soon as they do, everything looks and smells and feels different. It's very dark except for a torch on the wall. A gladiator, a different one, leans down to look into my face. His is scarred and dappled with blood. He smiles, and his teeth are nearly black. He speaks, and I am surprised to hear the question in English.

"Where did you get this?"

I am too scared to speak. My teeth are chattering uncontrollably. I feel cold like I've never felt before, permeating through my arms and shoulders and chest and stomach. I feel the need to throw up, and I'm pretty sure even my vomit is going to be cold.

"Little girl," he says again. "Where did you get this?"

"I...you speak English?"

All of the gladiator ghosts laugh, and the sound rings in the stone archway.

"We are dead, and you are nearly dead. You'll find out soon that we are not separated by language on this side of life. Now," he opens the pouch and plucks out the long gray bone inside, "where did you get this?"

My head is swimming. Is that why I could understand everything that was being said at the Bone Carnival? And what did he mean *you are nearly dead?* Fortunately, Grace answers for us both.

"She was tricked," she says quickly and with way more composure than me. "By a bad man. Can you help us? Take that to the other side? Keep it here with you?"

The gladiator turns to her, and then at the bone with an expression of curiosity on his face. "It's been so long since we've had visitors. People don't generally die here in the Flavian anymore. But what to do with those visitors when they show up with dark magic?"

"We didn't know it was dark magic," says Grace without hesitation.

"There is something in here that is offensive to our god, Jupiter. Humans—even very powerful ones— should not decide who lives and who dies. Yet the human whose body this bone came from seeks to do just that."

"Please," I say. I hate that my voice sounds so puny. "Help us get rid of it. Keep it here with you."

All the men in the tunnel scoff. The gladiator with the bone gingerly puts it back into its pouch and pulls its strings tight. "We cannot do that. I am not entirely sure what this magic is, but I know it's evil. It seeks to make an abhorrent bargain—the unnatural extension of life for one in exchange for cutting others tragically short." He frowns at me. "The realm of the dead is only separated by time, not space. If we keep this here with us, young ones, more like you, may die."

"But we're not dead," I say. "And I've had it for hours."

"Little one, you have death written upon your face," he says. "The look of one who will be joining us very soon, probably before tomorrow's sunrise. Do you really wish to gift that fate to someone else?"

"I don't want it for myself!" I say, and they all laugh, except the one with the bone, who looks at me and nods gravely. "How would you even know that?"

"Death has been a part of our existence from the very beginning," he says. "We lived a short time, over two thousand years ago, and have been here ever since. We know death."

"How do I stop it?" I ask, trying to keep the quiver out of my throat.

"I don't know this magic well. I think you'd do better to accept your fate than to try to fight against it. It may only drive you to madness and keep you there long after you're dead. I've seen that happen to many souls."

"Nobody is accepting this fate," says Grace. "Now what can we do?"

He grins at her and suddenly pats her on the back with his textbook-sized hand. "Ah, but I forget! The doomed one has a good friend. Maybe she's not so doomed after all, then."

"Just tell us!" I beg, a sob escaping my throat.

"It may come to nothing," he starts, "but part of what makes this bone unnatural is its separation from the rest of the body. There is pain here that was passed from parent to child, and he seeks to pass the pain along to you now, but it would be better if he found a way to make the pain stop with him. Since he is unwilling, the task falls to you. Find the body, restore the whole, and you may have a chance of survival. For now."

"What do you mean, for now?" I ask.

"No one can escape this fate forever," he says. "You will have to join us eventually. You, your family, everyone you know."

I nod. I knew that, of course, but I've never really thought about it like this.

Everyone I know will die. No one gets an exception—no one, expect maybe Gozzelino.

He gives the bone back to us. "Go. Restore the whole."

All of the gladiators line the entrance's walls to let us go back out into the arena. As we pass, some of them nod and others kneel. The air is unnaturally chilly, and when I put my hands into my pockets for warmth, I touch the missing child poster.

"Wait," I say, turning back. I take it out of my pocket and unfold it. "You said we had death written on our faces. Does he?"

The gladiator looks at the paper and considers my question. "This is only a likeness. Sensing death is only something you can do while seeing life; they may seem like opposites, but they're only two sides of the same coin. This," he gestures toward the paper, which suddenly feels flat and cold in my hand, "is only a thing. You are a life."

"But not for long," another voice toward the back, and the crowd of them chuckle.

"Go," says the giant man. "Good luck, little doomed ones. May Jupiter be with you."

We walk toward the light. And just when I'm thinking, oh no, I hope this isn't THE LIGHT, it all hits me: this is real. All of this is real. Magic is real. Ghosts are real. Death is real. It's too much to handle. I start shaking violently. I put a hand on the wall to steady myself, but my knees give out, and I sort of swoop to the ground.

Grace doesn't say anything, but she sits beside me, close enough that I can feel her warmth. *What have I done?*

At the end of the hall, I can see the outline of a person, but the light is too bright to make out who it is. I raise my hand to shield my eyes. And then a familiar voice calls out: it's my mom. The sound of her voice washes over me, comfort rushing in as a huge, overwhelming wave of relief.

"Mia?"

The initial comfort I felt at seeing Mom again is strong, but brief. Her face is stern, not happy like I want it to be. But before she can say anything, I burst into tears and melt into her arms.

She stays kind of stiff, and I want to shake her. I want to scream at her that I'm in danger. I don't do any of that. I feel too awkward and saying it out loud seems somehow treacherous.

"I found them!" she calls to someone behind her shoulder.

A group of adults come running to us—Mom, Dad, Dr. James, and Luca the historian-gladiator. Even though his costume looks authentic, now I know it's not at all. He looks like a pampered little king compared to those giant guys with rotting teeth. Enzo comes too.

"What happened?" Dad asks, but I'm already holding on tight to Mom, and I don't want to let go. Even though they don't show it like I want them to, I know they love me, and they'd be sad if I died at twelve years old. I don't want them to go through that.

Between us, I can feel a corner of the folded missing child flyer poke me from inside my pocket. Is he on the other side of life now too?

When we do finally break apart, I see Grace's mom is nervously rubbing her shoulder. Grace looks uncomfortable, and it makes me question myself: Am I overreacting? Enzo is always making fun of me for having no chill. How am I supposed to react to having a conversation with a hoard of terrifying ghosts who tell you you're about to join them? Why aren't our parents more relieved to see us?

"How did you two get separated from the group?" Dr. James asks.

"I don't really know. We stopped to talk for a second, and then when we looked up, you were gone," answers Grace. The lie comes out so effortlessly I can't help but be impressed.

Dr. James clenches her jaw and looks skyward, as if trying to keep herself from exploding, but Dad just says, "We found them. They're here now."

"Unfortunately I have to get going," says Luca. "You can take any exit, but the bus stop is over there, on the eastern end. Now that I have your numbers, though, I hope to see you again—maybe when I'm not wearing armor."

"We appreciate the tour, Luca." Mom still has her hands on my shoulders, but now she extends one to her friend. "We'll see you again soon."

I expect to get an angry lecture on the walk back to the bus, but Mom and Dad and Dr. James just keep talking to each other about the ancient Roman Empire, leaving me and Grace and Enzo alone. When I ask for my phone back, Mom takes it out of her purse and briefly tells me to keep it charged and with me so I can call her if I ever get lost again, and Grace's mom does the same.

When they turn their backs to us, though, Enzo takes his airpods out. He flicks his hair away from his eyes.

"Are you okay?" he asks without looking at me.

"Uh...yeah," I say. "I mean I'm okay now."

He nods, but doesn't look up from the ground. "Sometimes Mom and Dad aren't good at these things, but they were worried about you."

With that, he places his airpods back into his ears and quickens his pace. I'm still freaking out about my crash with the supernatural—and Enzo, strangely, has made me more sure of myself. How did he know to ask? How did he know Mom and Dad's response would shake me?

When I was in the fourth grade, I convinced Enzo to help me get into the attic. There's a tiny window up there that you can see from the sidewalk, but I'd never seen it from the inside, and I really wanted to go up there and see it from the other side. We did, and it turned out to be a dusty, hot mess up there, too much for even me. I was trying to get back down into the air-conditioned closet when I slipped from the beam, and my legs went through the floor, and I was stuck.

My legs dangled from the ceiling of Mom and Dad's closet as I continued to suffocate from the dusty attic heat from the waist up. It would have been funny if it wasn't so scary. Enzo couldn't get me down, so we had to call Mom and Dad. Mom came back from work early, but she couldn't get me down either, so Dad came home early too. Finally, Mom and Dad pushed while Enzo pulled me from above, and I was free. I laughed then, relieved and feeling like an animal finally free of a trap. Enzo laughed too, and he looked so funny with his face all red and his hair all wet from sweat that I just laughed harder.

It was just like an old sitcom on my app. *Leave It to Beaver* or *The Little Rascals.* All at once, I saw how ridiculous I must have looked with my legs kicking in the air above the closet, how silly it must have been to watch them disappear up the hole from below. Mom and Dad would surely climb up to join us soon, and we'd laugh together and hug like a black-and-white family on my Old Hollywood app.

Instead, I heard Dad say, "Well, I'm glad they're having a good time." But he didn't mean it.

"The only good thing about children," said Mom, "is that they eventually grow up."

The laughter stopped. Enzo looked at me just as my last giggle faded, and his eyes were worried.

As soon as we board the bus again, Grace slides into a seat and pulls me beside her.

"Give me your phone," she commands, and I hand it over. I don't feel like fighting or performing or bombasting anymore. I feel like hiding.

"There are two graveyards he could be buried in: Prima Porta or Cimitero Acattolico. I think 'acattolico' means 'not Catholic,' so that sounds right. I don't think a sorcerer would be Catholic." Grace's eyes are still glued to my phone's screen.

"Why did you have to use mine?" I ask.

"My mom sees my search history."

"Oh," I say. "My parents don't."

"I didn't think so. Anyway, Prima Porta is in the south, about ten kilometers from the city center, but the Cimitero Acattolico is only about a half a kilometer from the university, so we could even walk there." She lowers the phone and looks at me. "Do you think we could convince our parents to—"

"Wait," I say, "Who is in the cemetery? Why do you want to go there? And what is a kilometer?"

She blinks at me rapidly. "That gladiator ghost guy told us that we needed to reunite the bone with the rest of Gozzelino's body. If we can find out where his body is for sure, we can put the bone there and..I don't know, save your life?"

"Oh."

I want to cry. I have gotten myself into plenty of messes before but never this bad. Never anything that involved seeing and talking to dead people. Never anything that threatened my life. I keep thinking that maybe what we've seen today wasn't real, like it was some elaborate trick or maybe I just *thought* I threw the bone in the dumpster or maybe that I slipped on the ruins and hit my head and imagined the ghosts of gladiators. But with Grace here, it's really hard to pretend that what we've seen is anything other than terrifyingly real.

"And do you seriously not know what a kilometer is?"

"No, of course I know," I say, but I snatch my phone back and look it up ("a metric unit equal to .62 of a mile") while she talks at me some more.

"The problem is going to be how to actually find the grave itself and also how to reunite the bone with the body once we do find it."

"Can't we just put the bone on the grave? We don't have to actually..." I gulp, "dig him up, do we?"

She bites her lips together. I don't think either of us want to imagine it. She has the window seat, and she looks out for a moment. I nudge her shoulder.

"I guess one of us doesn't really have a choice," I say. "But I'll figure it out."

"We're in this together," she says slowly. Too slowly. She must be having doubts about being my friend.

I get out my phone and start searching.

"Look for some kind of information on grave tours in English," she says. "My Italian isn't good enough to read an Italian website, but maybe a tour guide would be able to point us in the right direction."

I nod, but I'm not interested in finding this stupid grave anymore. In the search bar, I type the question: *Can two people have the same hallucination?* And to my relief, I get a clear answer, yes. It's called *foile à deux* and according to the great and mighty Google, it's a shared delusional disorder in which "sometimes hallucinations are passed from one individual to another."

Grace is still talking, and I scroll. "I don't know how we're going to dig him up before nightfall, though. Do you think it's like, sunset, or more of like a midnight situation? Because if it's midnight, then—"

I stop and show her my phone screen. Her questions sputter to a stop as her eyes scan the Wikipedia page. "You think we're both having a mental illness episode?"

"I think we should tell our parents," I say.

"Really?"

"I really think we should tell them. They'll be able to...I don't know, take us to the doctor or something. Maybe they could give us some medicine so we don't see any more ghosts."

Her eyes get wide, but she closes her mouth and looks ahead to the seat in front of us. "I did wonder, when I was following you, whether or not something I didn't know about was happening in your head."

"I think it must be," I say. "I wish it wasn't true, but I don't know what else to believe."

"It wouldn't explain the luck," Grace says grimly. "The ice cream. The fire. Language camp being canceled."

"Could be coincidences."

"It's a possibility. And there wouldn't be any shame in it, either. Lots of people need help with brain chemicals misfiring. But is it also possible you're in denial?"

"What?"

"Denial. Like, you're trying to make something untrue by telling yourself that reality isn't happening."

"I don't know what that even means," I say. "All I know is that ghosts aren't real, and luck isn't real, and I

85

don't want to dig up a body just to not get mysteriously murdered when the sun goes down tonight."

"But we saw them," she whispers.

I think about the way Mom and Dad reacted to seeing me again, like they were just annoyed at the inconvenience, even when I started crying like a baby. "Did we?"

She clenches her jaw. "Look. It's your life, I guess. I could just let you believe that we're both having a simultaneous descent into mental illness, but I don't think that's what's happening, and I'd feel really bad if you got murdered tonight and I didn't do anything about it. So how about this: if we have another insanely lucky thing happen to us before this bus ride is over—like something that absolutely should not happen but does anyway—then we go to the cemetery. If not and the bus just drops us off at the university like it's supposed to, we tell our parents we're having vivid hallucinations, and we need them to help us."

It doesn't sound right. None of it does. Maybe I am in denial, like she said. Mostly when I screw up, I get my phone or tablet taken away for three days or however long it takes Mom and Dad to get tired of supervising without the help of a device. I've never actually been in real trouble before, and I don't like it.

The bus clunks and clatters under our feet, and with a harsh hissing sound, we pull over to the side of the road. Immediately people start shouting in Italian.

"What's going on?" I ask.

"I don't know, but..." She looks out the window: I see it too.

We've broken down right outside the entrance of the Cimitero Acattolico. And there's a little kiosk with a bored-looking teenager behind the counter under a sign that says in English "Tours."

The driver climbs aboard and says something. I know exactly what he's saying, but Grace translates anyway. "He says everyone needs to get out here. He also says he's glad this didn't happen on the bridge, because it's a long one, and we would have stopped traffic for miles."

Just as luck would have it. Gozzelino must not be able to control what kind of luck we get, because how else could we have broken down right in front of his final resting place?

10

All of us step off the bus, and of course, Enzo makes a beeline for the kiosk and takes a pamphlet.

"Dad," he calls out over his shoulder, "I think this is where that angel statue is on the Nightwish album cover."

"Oh, no way!" Dad snatches the pamphlet. The two of them have a thing for noisy foreign rock bands—but I have a feeling it's more about Dad trying to make Enzo happy than it is about the music, because most of those songs sound like garbage trucks crashing into broken glass factories. And he complained about Enzo's music a lot until the night of The Big Fight.

"You two should go see it," says Mom. "Dr. James and I can take the girls."

"I want to see the cemetery," I blurt. Mom, Dad, and Enzo all turn to stare at me.

"Me too," says Grace. "Can we go?"

"You don't even like Nightwish," says Enzo.

"Yes, I do."

"Oh yeah? What's your favorite song?"

I lick my lips and make myself look fully into his face. I don't know any of their songs, and he knows it, but I have to take a guess. What does their music even sound like, anyway?

"'Noise.'" I say with pretend confidence. It's a stupid answer, but he looks impressed.

"Oh," he says. "Yeah, 'Noise' is cool. You know the statue, then?"

"Yeah," I say. "I want to see it."

Mom and Dr. James talk for a moment, and they decide to go drink some wine and talk about economics while Dad, Enzo, Grace, and I sign up for the next tour. The statue is actually called *The Angel of Grief,* and it's the highlight of the tour, so we'll see it last, before all the graves of famous old poets and politicians and painters. I haven't heard of any of them.

Since we have a little time before the tour starts, we decide to wander through the graves a little.

"Stay where I can see you," says Dad. "And make sure you can see me."

The cemetery is expansive, but the entrance area is mostly flat, so that shouldn't be a problem. Our main question, now, is how we're going to find Gozzelino's grave. And that'll be the easier problem of the two problems to solve.

"I know this is scary," says Grace. "But...I'm surprised you thought this was a delusion. You don't really strike me as someone who gets scared easily."

I consider that for a second. "I don't normally. But I also don't normally have anything to be scared of. My parents aren't really strict like yours. When I get in trouble, it's usually not as bad. I guess once I figured out my parents couldn't actually kill me for whatever I did, I got a little...bold. I always thought I was brave, but I guess you can only be brave if you're willing to face something really scary. Now I know I'm not as brave as I thought."

"You're doing it, you know," she says softly. "I don't want to believe this is happening either, but it is, and we both know it, and we're both doing it. I think that makes us both pretty brave."

When I look up at her, she doesn't look at all like the sulking, angry Grace from this morning. Her eyes are honest, like she isn't afraid of telling me the truth. I know who the brave one is now. I want to fall into her arms and cry and let her take care of me, but I know that would scare her. She deserves to see strength too.

"Okay," I say. "Once we figure out where it is, we'll figure out a way to connect this bone with Gozzelino's body. We can do this."

"We can," she confirms and walks over to the kiosk. She and the teenager exchange a few words, and she ends up pulling out her phone. After a few minutes, she walks back over to me.

"The cemetery's gone high-tech," she says. "Apparently if you want to find a specific grave, all you have to do is download this app and search for it."

"Wow," I say. "Easy enough."

We wait, staring at the progress bar on her screen, waiting for it to reach 100%. When it does, she opens the app, selects the cemetery, and types "Gozzelino" into the search bar.

The app quits.

"What?" she says. She opens it again. Again, we wait.

She types "Gozzelino."

The app quits again.

"Are you serious?" she says. "Try it on your phone."

"Um...okay." I download it and select Cimitero Acattolico. This time, I look at the graves around me and type those names first. The names, locations, and pictures of the graves come up easily, no problem.

"What are you doing?" asks Grace. "We need to find—"

"Just trying something out," I say. After three ordinary searches, I type "Gozzelino."

My phone shuts off immediately. I don't like where this is going.

So much for Gozzelino not being able to control our luck. He's obviously not powerless in here, no matter who has his bone. Grace and I exchange dark looks.

"That answers several questions," she says. "Not only is Gozzelino real, but he really doesn't want us to find him."

"Well, too bad, because he's not going to win. Could you just ask that guy where the body is?" I say, nodding toward the teenager in the kiosk again.

"I did," she says. "He didn't know."

Now what?

"Okay, English tour!" the teenager says. "Starting now. Come, please!"

My dad waves us over, and we have no choice but to shuffle over to him. It's only the four of us plus one more couple, a retired couple in matching light-weight shirts, Boston Redsocks baseball caps, big puffy sneakers, and transition-lens glasses.

"Hi," the woman in the couple says to us. "Are you a Keats fan too?"

"Huh?"

"Keats, the famous English poet, was buried here."

"Oh. What did he write?" I ask.

They look at each other and shrug. "We're not sure," the man admits sheepishly. "But he's famous!"

They chuckle at each other, and I wish I were them—having a good vacation in Rome, not caring much about how they spend their time. As they turn and we walk through the graveyard, though, my sense of panic begins at my temples, with a tapping that I can hear in my ears, and moves to my chest, tightening my lungs and restricting my breath. Grace hears it.

"Mia," she whispers as the tour guide says some memorized sentences about a poet named Keats, who is evidently right below our feet, "breathe."

I have to look toward the treetops in order to be able to take a breath. Otherwise, it's just too much to know that the body I'm in right now will soon be where all other lifeless bodies go, into the earth, while the living trample around in their orthopedic shoes and take pictures of the stones above.

We go through the graveyard, and the tour guide points out the graves of famous Protestant Italians and ex-pats, like that poet, Keats. But I've never heard of most of them before, and the sense of dread and inevitability just seep through my body like a black smoke, choking me and clouding my thoughts. Finally, we approach a grave I assume must be the one Dad and Enzo want to see, because Enzo points and Dad takes his phone out to take a picture.

It is beautiful, in a tragic way. A life-sized angel kneels, draped over a grave, with its wings hovering over its back and its arms limply slung onto a stone table.

"*The Angel of Grief,*" the teenage tour guide says, "was made by the sculptor, William Wetmore Story, for his wife, Emelyn Story, in 1894. The full name of this work is *The Angel of Grief Weeping over the Dismantled Altar of Life.*

All who knew the couple said they were very much in love, and William was so devastated after his wife's death that he lost all interest in sculpting. But his children convinced him to make one last piece, and legend has it that he captured his own grieving spirit in the angel."

Capturing your own grieving spirit in a stone angel might sound kind of dramatic, but it makes me think about all the different ways people deal with being sad. Some people don't know what to do and end up making everyone around them sad too. Other people must somehow avoid starting a chain reaction in others. What was it the gladiator ghost said? There was pain in the bone, passed from parent to child, and now Gozzelino wanted to pass that pain along to more people. *It would be better if he found a way to make the pain stop with him,* he said. Is making a giant weeping angel statue making the pain stop with one person?

My dad, Enzo, and the tourist couple from Boston all take a few pictures.

"So cool," Enzo mumbles. "I wonder if Nightwish really came here to see it."

"Probably!" says Dad, but I'm sure he doesn't know.

"This way, please!" says the tour guide from over his shoulder, and the group moves in a herd to follow him.

But there's a tingly, prickly touch at the back of my neck. My hand immediately goes to scratch it, but then I feel a gust of wind, just like the one in the alley just before I saw the carnival. With the rest of the group walking away, I stop and turn.

The angel raises her head.

At first I can't really process what's happening. Then my heart freezes in my chest, mid-thump. It's like time has stopped.

Her face is stained with tears, and her loose bun is no longer stiff stone, but wild and askew, stone-colored but alive and dancing in the wind. She looks like she's been crying for a hundred years. Maybe she has been. She's looking straight at me.

I don't move. Every fiber in every muscle in my body is tensed. I'm not making this up. I didn't make up the gladiator ghosts, either. This is real.

Slowly, slowly, she looks toward an untrimmed rosebush. She lifts her arm. She points.

I turn toward the bush, growing wildly in the corner of the graveyard. Some—not many, but some— formerly-white roses cling to it, browned and bitten and wilted. I take one tiny step toward it and then look back at the angel. She's back to her former position, hunched over the grave and looking like she never moved.

An intense, involuntary shiver runs through me, and there's a feverish feeling right behind my eyes. I don't want to look, but I'm afraid the angel might spring back to life if I don't follow her directions. I look around for Grace, but she's gone on with the rest of the group.

Now that I take a closer look at the rosebush, there's something just behind it. I go to it and move some of the thorny branches away with my hand, and step inside. Deeper under the cover of the expansive growth, there's a gravestone almost as tall as I am engraved with a skeleton dancing under a moon and stars, and a name just below that:

GOZZELINO

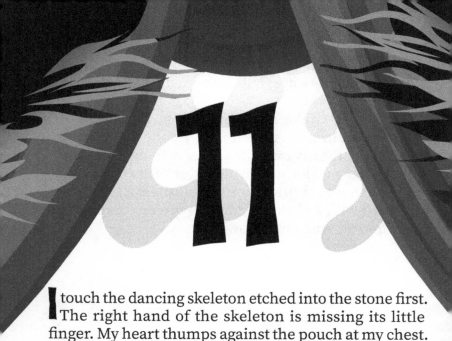

11

I touch the dancing skeleton etched into the stone first. The right hand of the skeleton is missing its little finger. My heart thumps against the pouch at my chest.

Under my feet, the grass barely grows, and the soft ground seems good for digging. I'm still not sure how we're going to do this, but at least the brush provides plenty of cover.

A hand clamps my shoulder.

I gasp and spin around to see the tourist man in the Boston Redsocks cap and his wife behind him, both with vacant expressions and dead eyes.

"*Va via!*" he says.

"I...don't speak Italian," I say. "Let's go back, and..."

But the man and his wife are already leading me, by my shoulders and elbows, back to the group.

"Only English?" asks the man, this time with an Italian accent. "How about a little poem, then?" he laughs darkly and hisses:

Darkling I listen and for many a time

I have been half in love with easeful Death

Now his wife laughs too and joins him, speaking the poem like an incantation:

Call'd him soft names in many a mused rhyme
to take into the air my quiet breath
Now more than ever seems it rich to die
To cease upon the midnight with no pain
While thou art pouring forth thy soul abroad
In such ecstasy!

"You like it?" snarls the man. "It's by a local. John Keats."

I scream and kick and struggle against them, but nobody notices, and I can't figure out why nobody would see a nice-looking tourist couple drag me here reciting poetry they claimed not to have known just minutes ago. But then I notice the expression on the rest of their faces: Dad, Enzo, Grace, and the tour guide all have the same weird, empty looks on their faces. It's that look people get when they're watching tablets. It's the look that means they're not really here.

There's nobody else around. The bustling Roman streets are not far, but they may as well be, with the high stone walls of the cemetery encircling us and trapping me inside with...well, these people aren't the friends and family and kindly strangers they were just a minute ago. Where did they go? How do I get them back?

"Dad!" I shout. "Enzo! Dad!"

We're still walking in the graveyard with Grandma and Grandpa Tourist on either side of me, squeezing my arms with very non-grandparent-like strength. We're all still following the hollow-faced tour guide, and we seem to be walking with a purpose now.

We round a corner and head straight up a hill toward a small, one-person mausoleum. The stones are blackened with age, and a forest green door stands between two pillars.

"Wait," I say, but none of them look back at me.

Grace, Dad, Enzo, and the tour guide part and line up to make an aisle for me. The couple continue to drag me by my arms up the hill.

"Wait," I say, this time more urgently.

The green door swings open, and a gust of cold wind escapes the tomb and hits my face. The feverish feeling spreads through my entire body.

"Wait!"

What happens next is a total fluke. I have no idea what is happening or what to do—the only thing I know is that this bone is causing all this trouble, and a burst of anger gives me the strength to grab the pouch with my hands. I fumble for the little bone, which feels like a small pencil through the velvet. In one motion, I snap it in half.

The couple immediately lets go.

I fall to the ground.

"Oh," says the man in the now fully-dark transition lenses. He helps me to my feet. "I'm sorry."

"Did something happen?" asks his wife. "Did we bump you, honey?"

I'm still in a state of shock, so I just kind of shake my head. Luckily, Grace swoops in.

"Maybe she needs some water. I fell down once when I was dehydrated last summer."

"Yeah," says my dad. "I think we could all use a little hydration."

"Mm-hm," agrees Enzo. "I feel weird."

The tour guide thanks us for coming and asks if we have any questions, but nobody has any, and he's asked the question in a way that tells me he's in no state to answer anyway.

"Okay," Grace says, pulling me by my elbow. I wince; she doesn't know that I have a burgeoning bruise there. "What happened?"

I tell her about the angel, the rosebush, the grave, the zombie faces on everyone, and the mausoleum. To her credit, she listens to everything and doesn't interrupt, even though saying it all out loud sounds ridiculous, even to me. When I get to the part about breaking the bone, she squints and bites her lip.

"And how is it now? The bone?"

I don't even have to feel it to know. I put my fingers on the velvet and of course, it's whole again.

"Okay," I say, "Well, the good thing is that I know where his grave is now. And if there's no one else around to control, maybe I could put the bone with the body by myself."

"I'm coming with you," says Grace. "I've already asked my mom if I can spend the night with you, and she said it's fine as long as your mom says yes. We can sneak out after dinner and come back here to dig him up."

I nod, grateful for once to have a friend whose mind can keep up with mine. Back at home, I'm the one making all the plans, and my friends are the ones trying to talk me out of it or whining about all the trouble they'll get in if and when we get caught. Sneaking into an historic graveyard to dig a body up is probably the most trouble I've ever risked before, but what's the alternative?

"We're going to need some tools," I say.

"Like those?" Grace gestures to a little shed, where, for some reason, a pickaxe and a shovel are leaning against the side.

I grin. "Lucky."

She takes my hand and squeezes. "Lucky"

12

Mom says no to a sleepover the first time, but then when I point out that it would let her be the first to give Dr. James "a break," (parents love "breaks" from their kids) she agrees. Mom collects favors from her friends like some people collect cookie jars. Grace comes home with us, and we order takeout from one of the places on the block—some kind of vegetable soup with pasta in it. In the US, this kind of soup comes from a can, tastes like metal, and the pasta basically falls apart on your tongue, but in Italy, it tastes like a spicy garden. The homemade pasta inside is the crown jewel, and each piece tastes like it was put there as a gift to the soup. We also eat crunchy, crusty bread and butter, still soft and warm on the inside, and salad with tomatoes, redder and fuller and tastier than any other tomato I've ever eaten before. I probably should be nervous about the task ahead of us, but food this good has a certain magic to it, and it's impossible not to enjoy dinner. I wonder, as I pop another one into my mouth, whether this is the luck at play or if it's just Italy.

After dinner, Grace and I go into my room and shut the door. The sun is lower in the sky.

"Should we take anything?" she asks.

"I think we have to get going," I say, gesturing at the sky.

I try to only think about the task ahead, not my family. If I believe I may never see them again, I'll never leave. *Just one step at a time. Immerse yourself.*

The fire escape is a little tricky to figure out, but thankfully, it's quiet enough once we do. I climb down first and then Grace.

"Pdrr-roul?" comes a sweet sound from behind me on the street.

My little furry friend is back. "Wish us luck, little guy," I say while he smashes his head against my hand. "I'll be back later. Look after..." I look up at the window, and a lump rises in my throat.

"Let's go," says Grace.

"That's his hungry meow. Maybe I should feed him before—"

"Mia, we need to go now. Come on," says Grace, and we start off. The cat sits under the ladder and watches us leave. I get the feeling he wants us to stay, but Grace is right; the sun is setting fast, and we have work to do.

We go down onto the street and walk quickly towards the graveyard. While we walk, the bone seems to become heavier, making the cord dig into the skin on the back of my neck. Dark clouds cover the sky above our heads.

Leaves swirl in the wind around our feet as we walk. Shopkeepers pull down their awnings and waiters help their al-fresco patrons carry in their wine and water glasses as the wind picks up, now mixed with tiny, sideways raindrops.

A lady on the street says something to us. Grace answers her.

"She said we'd better get home," Grace says and looks up at the angry sky. "There's a storm coming."

"Yeah, you don't have to be fluent in Italian to know that," I say. I wish we could go home. I love thunderstorms when you're inside, cozy and warm, while the weather rages just outside the window. I love sitting on our front porch in Louisville during storms too. Something about watching how manically the trees rock back and forth in the sky makes me scared in a fun way. The best is when it's early fall, just a little chilly, and I can wrap a blanket around me, read a book, and listen to the sound of the raindrops hitting the roof.

This is nothing like that. In an instant, Grace and I are pummeled by rain that blows in in sheets. We're both dressed in tank tops, shorts, and sneakers, so there's nothing to do but to accept the fact that we're already soaked beyond saving. I run my fingers through my hair to slick it back against my head, but Grace's hair hangs down and clings to her back, longer and darker than ever.

Lightning strikes just as we cross the gate, and the brief light makes me realize just how dark it's gotten. Though the sun is hidden behind the thick clouds, it can't have set yet because I'm still here. But it's unnerving not to know exactly how much time we have. If I'd have been smarter, I'd have looked up the time of sunset before leaving, but we wouldn't know what time it is, anyway—our phones are at home. I guess they'd have been completely destroyed by water damage by now even if we had remembered them.

I'm having a hard time thinking of things like that as luck anymore, though.

We take the pickaxe and the shovel as we pass by the gate, and it seems to me that I'm just watching myself do this, as if I'm not in my body anymore. I'm not sure what Grace is even doing here. Why should she be here, soaking wet and about to be in trouble for the rest of her life, just for me? I've known her for exactly one day, but I've already never had a friend like her before. *If I make it,* I vow, *I'll be more like her. I'll be this kind of friend.*

We find the grave near the bramble by the wall. I untangle the rosebush so Grace can get through, dragging the pickaxe behind her.

Something jumps out of the brush. My entire body jolts before I recognize what it is: the cat. My cat. It takes me a second to see that he's the same black cat with the star on his chest and the white on his toe because he's lost all of his friendliness. His fur stands on end, even when wet, and he arches his back to let out a loud hiss.

"It's okay, little guy," I say, bending down and reaching out my hand. "Look, it's me!"

He lets out a deep warning growl.

I shake my head in disbelief. "What's the matter with him?"

"This must be a different cat," says Grace. "Now let's go."

"No, it's definitely him. Look, he has that tiny white mark on one toe—"

"Get out of here!" Grace tries to shoo him away, but he won't budge.

"It's okay, little one," I say. "We just need to get past you, okay?" I nudge him with my foot, and scratches my leg. "Ow!"

The scratch burns like it's on fire, but it only lasts for a second.

"Shoo!" Grace claps her hands right in front of his nose, and he backs away. "Get out of here!"

"Grace! No!"

"That mangy cat attacked you!"

He's already running through the cemetery—a little black streak sprinting through the gravestones.

"Well," I say, looking after him, "I'll make sure he's okay after—"

"After we make sure *we're* okay," she finishes for me.

At first, it feels like what we're doing is truly impossible. How can two girls with some found garden tools possibly do what we need to do here? But neither of us mention the inevitability of failure. We work silently, slowly unearthing the ground below us. I just concentrate on what's right in front of me, moment by moment. Shovel this dirt out. Now shovel that dirt out. Our pile grows bigger and bigger.

As I dig, though, I feel stranger and stranger. Like my breath is leaving my lungs and just becoming part of the air around me, colder and mixed with the rain.

"Grace?"

"Yeah," she says, not taking her eyes from the hole she's digging.

"I don't...feel great."

Her head snaps up, and her expression changes in an instant. "I don't want to scare you," she says slowly. "But you don't look great, either."

"What's happening to me?"

"You're...fading."

I drop the shovel and bring my hands to my face. They have changed—they're ghostly white, and I can see the dirt piles on the other side of them.

"Don't stop," she says, picking up my shovel and handing it to me.

How is this the same girl who wouldn't sneak out to get breakfast for herself this morning? I don't feel like fighting this anymore, but her demand, her conviction, has an effect on me, and I keep shoveling.

Suddenly, Grace's pickaxe hits something hard. The bump comes just before another loud crash of thunder, and the two of us share a significant look, water raining down our faces. I use the shovel to scrape off the dirt from the door of a coffin.

As we scrape and shovel to completely expose the coffin, the strange feeling gets worse. I suck on my loose tooth, hard, but it stays in place. "Grace," I say, feeling ashamed of the misery in my voice, "I don't think I can do this."

She's trying to be brave, but I can tell she wants to run. Instead, she stretches her trembling hand, palm up. "I'll do it. Give me the bone."

I feel like I don't have a choice. I want to run away, throw up, and faint all at the same time. I take the pouch from my neck and hand it to her. She loops it around her own neck.

She looks me up and down. "You should sit down."

"You can't do this by yourself."

She bites her lip and looks down. When she speaks, her voice is barely louder than the rain. "Let me try."

She reaches down with both hands and grabs the top of it. "It's not nailed down," she says. "I think it'll just swing open. I'm going to do this fast. It's the right hand, right?"

My breath is so shallow now that I can barely get the words out. "Right."

She fishes the bone out of the pouch. It's even more grotesque than I imagined, and smaller too—just an ivory-colored twig streaked with brown decay. The way Grace holds it is the way I imagine a surgeon would hold a knife or a hunter would hold a bow—it's just a tool in her hands, and she is the determined wielder.

"Okay," she says. She looks different now, more vibrant. There's a subtle glow that's coming from the inside of her chest that I never noticed before. Is the change coming from her, or me?

She raises her hand with the bone inside above the coffin and opens the lid. From where I sit on my dirt pile, the first thing I see is a skeleton hand, still in a sleeve with velvet that looks as if it were cut from the same cloth as the pouch.

It's only still for a brief moment.

It strikes out and grab Grace's wrist. Grace screams.

Though I try to make it to my feet, I'm too weak now—my body refuses to obey my mind. I am crumpled on the ground while I watch the terror deepen in Grace's face, and she struggles against the rotting corpse inside.

And it pulls her in.

It pulls her in.

13

F or a horrible moment, time freezes.

No thinking.

No breathing.

Nobody else around.

The wind howls through the thicket and hits my face, and I come to my senses, just barely. I crawl on my hands and knees toward the edge of the hole we've dug and look inside. A blackness seems to go on forever, like the hole leads right down into the center of the earth.

"Grace?" I call, and the darkness swallows up my voice so it sounds like I'm calling into a pillow. There's no answer.

My mind races through possibilities: Do I jump down? Call for help? Go back to the apartment, the last place we were safe and secure and dry and warm and hope she somehow is back there?

As much as I want to, I can't deny what I just saw. It's my fault Grace ended up with the bone, and it's my fault they took her. *They*. I shudder. I know exactly who took her. It was Gozzelino.

If we can somehow reunite the bone to his body—I don't know how we can, but if we can—I have a feeling we'll be okay. It's the one thing he told the first boy he entrapped never to do, and so it's the thing that must be done. But the grave is deep and dark, and I'm not sure what will happen if I try to go down there.

I take a pebble from the ground and drop it inside. It's true the rain is still raging, but I can't hear it hit the bottom. I gulp. I know what I have to do, but...

No, a not-often-used voice of reason chimes inside me. *No, no, no, no—*

But Grace is in there, somewhere, hopefully still alive. She could have walked away from me at any point, but she stayed to help me. She snuck out of my apartment with me, walked through the pouring rain, and helped me dig up a monster. I can't leave her here.

Trembling, I swing my legs around until they're dangling over the edge of the grave. Lightning flashes overhead, but it doesn't touch the darkness beneath my feet. In a horrible instant, I realize the sun has set. I'm out of time.

One.

I inhale deeply though my nose. The heavy rain-scented air fills me.

Two.

I curl my fingers into the dirt beside me, clawing and raking it into my palms, clutching tight to what I know is real.

Three.

I jump.

14

I land sooner than I thought I would, as if it was really just a six-foot-deep empty hole in the ground. The soft earth catches me as I land on my feet with my knees bent. I look down and see my feet.

Wait.

I see them. How is there enough light to see my feet?

I look up at the sky—it's daylight now, and the sky above me is overcast. There's nothing in the grave with me—no coffin, no body, no mouldy-jacket-clad skeleton swiping at the air to capture me.

The top of the grave is a few feet above my head, but there's a looped root sticking out that I can wedge my foot inside. I prep and jump, stretching out my arm, and my fingers clutch the sun-warmed grass above. But the root snaps, and I grip with all of the arm strength I can muster while kicking my legs into the air below.

I've almost pulled myself up when my hand slips, and I fall just an inch back into the grave. And then, without warning, there is a blast of cold on my arm. I gasp and look up.

It's not Grace; it's a boy. And it's not just any boy—it's the boy from the carnival. Though I couldn't piece it together there, it's clear now: he's the same boy from the poster too.

Missing.

Not anymore, I guess.

He grasps my arm with his icy fingers and helps to pull me up. We work together as I scramble out and onto the grass. I am too afraid to move, so I sit, frozen on the warm ground while he quietly waits beside me.

I don't want to look at him, but I can feel him there beside me. I just know he's watching me, the same way you walk into a room and know right away that people were telling secrets to each other. The air is thickly charged with the knowing, the certainty.

I'm not in the graveyard anymore. I'm in a field that has been transformed. I'm just outside of a circle of tents, striped in dull colors. There's a pipe organ playing something from within that tent circle—a song that might sound happy if not for the fact that the organist had slowed down the tempo to that of a funeral march. And though the sun is shining, there is a purple smoke, hazy and thick, coming from the tents.

After a long pause, the waiting is more excruciating than whatever is to come, and I turn my head slowly to look at him. The boy is wearing a pale gray hoodie that matches his face and faded blue jeans.

"You almost did it, you know," he says. "He even had to go back into your world to try to scare you away." He points to the cat scratch on my leg. "If the sun hadn't set, you'd probably have both gotten away. I'm Valerius, by the way. You can call me Val."

CHAPTER 14

There are a million questions swarming my mind, but the one I blurt out is, "Where are we?"

"You're inside the Bone Carnival now," he says.

"Is this real?"

"It's real; we're just on a different plane. He uses his magic to keep us in here when we die. I'm not sure where you go if you die and you're not here, but I know one thing: we're all dead, and he is alive, but just enough to gather the years from one more child."

"If you're dead, does that mean I'm dead too?"

He points to my heart. I look down. There's an eerie, yellowish-green glow shining just under my still-pink skin. "You're not, not yet. You're fading fast, though. You'll be dead in a few hours."

I gulp. "And Grace?"

"The girl you were with? Oh, yes. She's dead."

A stabbing feeling in my heart makes me cry out. *No. It can't be true. She was just with me. He's mistaken.* "Where is she?"

He points to the collection of tents. "Over there. They've already started the process."

"What process?"

"Taking her soul out. He'll take her body back, and she'll be found on the other side. In your world. It's what happened to all of us—or will. Mine still hasn't technically been found yet."

Without waiting for further instructions, I bolt toward the tents.

"Hey!" he calls, and quickly—too quickly—catches up with me. "I wouldn't try to—"

"You said she was dead!" I shout. When I get to one of the tents, I slash open the canvas with the side of my hand, but no one's in that one. I move to the next one, ripping it open, my arm moving with a strength I didn't know I had.

"She is! See this smoke?"

"Yeah. What about it?" I dart to the next one and snatch at the opening, but she's not there either.

"Do you smell it?"

I stop and look at him. What could he mean by that? Against my intuition, I inhale the air, expecting it to smell burnt and vaguely chemical, kind of like sparklers on the Fourth of July. Instead, it smells cool, like peppermint. Like...

"Grace," I whisper.

"Yes."

I reach out my hand and put it into the purple peppermint-scented cloud, and it dances between my fingers in wispy bursts, warmer than the air around it.. The song has stopped, and now the quiet of the long, empty plain is somehow much louder than the pipe organ ever could have been. The circle of tents sway mildly in the breeze.

I don't want to know, but I have to ask. I gesture to the cloud. "What is this?"

The boy takes a step toward me, like he wants to touch me but thinks better of it. "It's her. It's the rest of her life she would have lived if she'd never—"

"If she'd never taken the bone," I finish for him. "If *I'd* never taken the bone." I bury my face in my hands, crushed by my own shame. I can't say the words because my throat is closed and my tongue is lead, but they ring through my head, heavy and inescapable.

It should have been me.

15

Val reaches out a hand and awkwardly pats my shoulder. "It's okay," he says.

We're hidden behind one of the tents, so I guess I could cry if I needed to, but I don't. Instead, I stop, blink, and ask: "It is?"

"Well," he scratches his head and looks uncomfortable. "No, I guess it's not. And it's especially not now, now that you're here. Because you'll be next. But truly, it's not all that bad! There's cannoli here, and games, and—"

"Back up, ghost boy." Something about that last statement awoke some sort of animal instinct in me: a need to survive. I have to get back, and I am not going back alone. "What do you mean, 'I'm next?'"

"I just mean once he's finished with your friend— Grace, is it?—he'll come for you, now that you're here."

My curiosity is in battle against my fight-or-flight instincts. I want to ask him about a million more questions but the one that bubbles up is: "How do I get out of here?"

He raises his arms in a half-hearted shrug. "If I knew that..."

He doesn't have to finish for me to understand. Of course he wants out too—he obviously has family on the other side who care that he's missing.

"Okay," I say. *What do I do when I'm sure I'm going to get in trouble and want to delay it to work out a new plan?* "Hide me. I'm going to save Grace and bring her back. If you help me, I'll bring you back too."

"There's no bringing me back," he says, pointing to his chest. Where mine is glowing faintly, his is cold, gray, and empty. "But...there is something you could do for me."

"What?" I say, unable to hide my desperation. "Say it."

But at that moment, children begin to pour out of one of the tents. Val grabs my hand and pulls me behind the puppet theater where the two hand puppets beat each other with clubs earlier. "Go inside," he says, and I slide behind the stage where the puppeteers would sit. It's a tight squeeze, but I fit. And then he comes in behind me, and the space feels so tight that I have to think about my breathing. I work hard to keep it slow and steady, so nobody hears us. There's a small space between the sides of the little box where I can see the opening of the tent everyone is exiting. More and more children shuffle out, most dressed in ancient clothing, and finally, one bigger boy comes out holding a limp body in his arms. Although her head is hidden by his arm, I can tell from the long black hair hanging down that it's Grace.

How am I going to get her out of here?

He sets her down on the ground in front of the tent. I almost don't see what comes next because I'm so focused on Grace. Something black flickers against the tent, and I squint and press my face closer to the crack between the boards.

With the gait of a king, the little black cat walks behind the boy carrying Grace. Without breaking stride, he transforms, starting with his feet. Within two steps, he is no longer a cat; he is the slim man in the back cape and dark ponytail from the carnival.

"That's Gozzelino," Val whispers. "Did he come to your window? Did you follow him into the carnival too?"

It all seems so obvious now, of course. Memories flash like scenes behind my eyes: the cat coming to my window, leading me to the Bone Carnival, getting touchy every time I touched his paw, trying to keep me and Grace away from the grave. I cannot believe I fell for it. I didn't think my shame could get any sharper; I was wrong.

When I don't answer, he says, "That's how he got me. I think he senses when kids are lonely."

I can't take my eyes off Grace. It should be me lying lifeless on the ground there, not her. It's not fair.

Or maybe not lifeless—one last puff of purple smoke escapes her lips, and the man hovers over her, inhales, and raises his arms triumphantly.

"Another seventy years of the carnival guaranteed for us, my friends!" He looks over the crowd of children who cheer at his announcement. "Though she is not the guest we were expecting, she has provided us with more time together, and so I hope you'll be kind to our newest arrival when she awakes. She is one of us now, having made the ultimate sacrifice. Let her rest for now, and then later, give her a warm welcome!"

They cheer again. I take advantage of the noise to ask one of the million questions swarming my mind.

"Val," I say, poking him in his cold ribcage, "what does me mean, 'when she awakes?'"

"He just took the rest of her years she would have lived. Her spirit is still alive; it's trapped here now. She just needs some time to rest before waking up again—kind of like recharging her batteries." He shakes his head sadly. "This is the first time I've really seen it for myself. They just did this to me last week."

"Wait," I say with the beginnings of an idea forming, "you've only been here one week?"

"Six days," he says.

The crowd quiets again, so we watch closely. Gozzelino snaps his fingers, and some of the children go fetch instruments and begin playing. Some start dancing. It's not the kind of dancing that kids at my school back home do at the Fun Friday dances: at those, the boys and girls divide themselves on opposite sides of the gym and just jump up and down to music. Here, the dancing is closer and wilder with more spinning and swinging, completely lacking any shyness or self-consciousness. Soon, all of them are joining in. The boy who carried Grace to the center of the circled tents carries her to the side so she doesn't get trampled. It seems odd to me because if they're ghosts, wouldn't their feet go right through?

I remember the lessons we were taught about misinformation in school: everything I thought I knew about ghosts is learned from secondhand sources. But

I have Val with me, and he seems friendly. And only here for six days...that means his Mom was handing out flyers at the Vatican on day four. She must have had more faith in church-goers and sight-seers than in the *Agenzia Informazioni*. And then the memory comes back to me: *carnival stano* and a sketch of a boy in the police notebook.

It was Val.

"I have to get to her," I tell him. "And personally kick Gozzelino in the teeth while I'm at it."

He snickers. "Wouldn't we all?"

But I wasn't kidding. I shove him, pushing aside my surprise about ghosts and their ability to be shoved at all—those notions I had before were wrong, I guess—and march out toward the circle of the dead dancing children. Swiftly, I take a stick from the ground and launch it at Gozzelino's back. It falls short and misses him; he doesn't even turn around.

Something grabs the back of my shirt and pulls me back into the puppet theater.

"Are you crazy?" Val hisses when they two of us are safely crammed back inside. "Do you know what you've got to lose?"

"So what?" I ask. "You said I was mostly dead anyway."

"Mostly dead isn't all-the-way dead, believe me." He touches the center of his chest, dull and gray where a little light shines in mine. "And maybe if you're not all-the-way dead, there's a way you could help."

I look back at Grace, still limp on the ground while the ghost kids all party around her in the peppermint-scented air. Gozzelino seems to have gone inside his tent.

"I need to get her out," I say bluntly.

"Impossible."

"Audrey Hepburn says nothing is impossible. The word itself says 'I'm possible.'"

"That is the dumbest thing I've ever heard," says Val evenly in that slow, patient voice grown-ups usually use with kids. "You can't get her out alive because she's dead. But that doesn't mean you still can't help us."

I start to ask another question, but he clasps his hand over my mouth with surprising strength and looks over his shoulder. "Not here," he says. "We need to find another place to regroup. Then I'll tell you everything."

16

Val won't say anything until we're safely out of sight because he's still mad at me for throwing the stick at Gozzelino. He and Grace would get along just fine. They'd probably both be out of here already if it were her helping him and not me. That thought makes me feel like I'm back in school in Louisville, in a group project with two kids that are way smarter than me, which, if I'm being honest, isn't a rare situation. In that scenario, I know my role: I'm the one who sits back and makes jokes. But with the stakes this high and the tiny detail that I'm the only one technically *alive*, I don't really have that option.

To get out, here's what he does: Val joins the kids for a few dances, asks the band to play a song everyone evidently loves, dances with them for another minute, and then signals to me to run behind the tents and into the tree line. He told me to hide behind a tree once I got to the first one, which I do. Once I hide behind the first tree, though, I realize that what seems like a dense forest is truly just a few trees: and on the other side, unbelievably, is the carnival again.

I walk through the trees in astonishment. Yes, it's definitely the same carnival, with the same tents, the same band, the same lifeless Grace tossed aside in the circle like dirty laundry on the bathroom floor.

"Stop!"

Val rushes to my side, panting. "Don't go any farther, or you'll be on the other side!"

I decide to take a step back and follow his advice. "How—?"

"We're in...I guess it's kind of like another dimension. Reality layered on top of reality. But the two worlds are the same in all the basic ways."

"What do you mean?"

"Like...the world we were born in was really big. You could walk in one direction for a really long time, but then—"

"You'd be back where you started," I say, his meaning clicking together for me. "Does this mean this world is really small?"

"Yeah. I think there are others, because sometimes Gozzelino threatens to send kids to another one if they misbehave and talk to the live ones, like you, but he created this one, and it's only as big as he needs it to be." He kicks at a pebble on the ground. "I think these trees are just for decoration, because he doesn't like to remember that there's nothing here except the carnival."

"Why does he need this?" I ask, gesturing around. "What does he get out of it?"

"With his magic, he can take the remaining years of people who are alive. So this place serves two purposes: it's a trap to capture people whose lifespans he can syphon and a safe to store the souls of those same people." He frowns and shrugs. "At least, I think that's it. I haven't been here very long, and none of the others will talk to me, so I've been having to figure things out on my own."

"Why won't they talk to you?"

"I don't really know," he says, grabbing onto a branch and looking out at the carnival thoughtfully. "I think it's because he got lots of years out of his first batch of kids; they've been here a long time. Almost five hundred years. This carnival is really the only life they know. And they think I'm really stupid for following the cat here," he adds sheepishly.

"I guess we're both stupid, then." It does make me feel a little better that I wasn't the only one who was duped. "But why does Gozzelino want all of these lives?"

"He needs the energy to finish that medicine. He says it'll only take a little while longer, and once he does, he'll cross over into another world. A better one."

"Heaven?"

"Maybe. But I think he's scared. If he was going to make this medicine, he'd have done it by now, right?" Val lets go of the branch and looks at me as if he just can't help feeling sorry for both of us. "He's probably been going around disguised as a cat to lots of kids, but we were the only two dumb enough to follow him."

"Enough calling each other dumb, okay?" He may be able to withstand lots of flogging for the same mistake, but I have to move on. I get enough of that from other people—I can't do it to myself. "You said you wanted help."

"Right." His face is downcast, like he'd temporarily forgotten that I wasn't there to stay. "So when I was... taken, I'd asked my mom to take me to see the Travoli fountain. I'd lived in a small town just south of Rome my whole life and still hadn't seen it. Mom was afraid of the city, like, because of all the people. She hated crowds. She kept saying the only people besides tourists in Rome were the people trying to take advantage of them. She said she'd even heard on the news once that some kidnap children and blackmail the families. It's why we never traveled before, or spent a holiday more than an hour away—she was too afraid. So when we finally did go into the city, I saw the carnival and thought it was normal. And then I was chosen to carry the bone, and I felt like I was really lucky.

"Until sunset," I murmur.

He nods. "Just my bad luck—it was very near sunset already. I could have gone back to her right away, but I was having such a good time, and the music was just...I felt like I wanted to stay forever." He sighs and looks down at his hands. "There was a parade, and because I was carrying the bone, they put me in the king's throne and carried me down the street. When we got closer to the cemetery, I could tell something was wrong because the closer we got, the heavier the bone got, until it was so heavy I couldn't move anymore. The kids started talking to me then, telling me I was about to come play with them forever, but I must be careful to not let the bone touch the body. I tried to run away, but the bone was too heavy, and they just watched me try to get away and laughed. They brought me to the grave and dumped me. I thought I was going to land on the ground, but instead *he* came out of the ground and dragged me under." He pauses and looks at me.

Sometimes when someone tells a story, the way they tell it gives away just how much they needed to get it out. Val's story was like this; I still didn't know how to help, but I had a feeling listening to him was more helpful than it probably seemed. Nobody has ever called me a good listener, but I've told stories like this before, desperate for someone—anyone—to listen to me. Because of this, I wait.

Eventually, he lets out a heavy sigh. "I need you to go back and tell my mom what happened to me. Gozzelino goes back into the world, both as a cat and as a man, and he put my body under a bridge. He goes there every day to check and see if anyone has found it yet, but it's still there. If I help you get back, can you just tell someone that it's there? My mom...I need her to know."

I am speechless. I can't imagine being separated from my body, worrying about my family like that. I want to scream, to shout that it isn't fair, to hug him. But the best I can manage is a stunned nod.

He smiles weakly. "Thanks. I guess you'll have to find out where they put Grace's body too. They might put hers next to mine, and then it'd be pretty easy for you, right?"

My stomach sways. "If I lead the police under a bridge to find two dead bodies—including my friend's—they're going to have some questions for me."

He frowns. "I didn't think of that. Yeah, I guess they might."

"And," I say, "if he's drained your remaining years, technically those years still exist. They're just transferred to him, right?"

I can tell he's confused. "Right."

"And if you've only been here six days, your body's still there in the outside world, right?"

He twists his face. "Are you saying—"

"I'm not saying I know for sure," I say, "but I think we could still pull this off."

He stares at me, his face revealing nothing. Maybe he's afraid to hope.

"You said it yourself—your spirits aren't dead; they're just trapped. If we can destroy this world, we might be able to get your spirit to your body. You don't have to be scared to try," I add quickly. "If we're wrong, I'll go to the police. I'll tell them where your body is. I'll make sure your mom finds out. I can even go to your funeral. And you'll be no worse off than you were before Grace and I came. But if I'm right and restore the bone to Gozzelino's body, you can go back and tell your mom what happened yourself."

He is quiet for a long time. Finally, he looks back at the carnival, at the silhouettes of the children against the dark-gray sky, dancing with all of their might and never getting tired. "It won't be easy. I don't even know where he keeps the bone when he isn't using it to lure kids here."

"We'll find it. We have to." I reach out and touch his arm, which is cold. "There's nobody coming to save us."

He bites his lip. "I guess there are some good things about having nothing left to lose. But promise me one thing."

"Okay," I say eagerly. I just need him to help me get Grace back.

"We won't do anything that will risk your life. You're already fading, and if you get worse, you go home. You tell my mom what happened. We can't let Gozzelino or any of the kids know that you're here, and you can't do anything stupid again."

I nod. Now that I think about it, throwing that stick was pretty stupid.

"Good," he says. "Now let's go get your friend."

17

Here's the plan: Val thinks the grave is the portal to the real world, and now that the bone is here with Gozzelino and not tethered to me anymore, we should just be able to jump in. We'll go get Grace and hope nobody follows us.

Even I have to admit that hope is a bigger factor here than it should be, but time is of the essence, and it's the only plan we could agree on.

"I can see why *you're* here," says Val, teeth clenched, when he finally agrees that we should at least try. "You don't love thinking things through, do you?"

I sigh and watch as he struggles to climb up the tree. "We are *going* to get out, and when we do, you and Grace should get married. That way, right after you thank me for saving your lives, you can go back to insulting me in unison. And in Italian."

That quiets him down. I climb up after Val, and we wait there in the branches, a few feet from each other, while the rest of the camp settles down and goes to sleep. There are a few lanterns hanging outside of the tents with candles inside, but one by one the candles go out, the circle empties, and the only light is from the moon and stars overhead.

Val settles with his back against the tree, and I do the same. I rub my eyes.

"Don't fall asleep," he says.

"I won't," I say, but it's hard. I just got over my jet lag, and now it's late into the night. But the only thing worse than falling asleep in a tree and potentially falling would be missing our opportunity to get Grace back home. I don't think I could go back without her if I tried. Besides the fact that I'd definitely be suspect number one when the police found her body, I need her unlike I've ever needed a friend before; she's so different than anyone else I've ever met. She challenges me, she pushes me, she makes me better. She followed me when Gozzelino made me act all weird when I was chasing the cat to the Bone Carnival. I want her to be back and live a good life no matter what, but I really want her in my life too.

I imagine where she is right now, in one of the tents, maybe just waking up, maybe just meeting these kids who have been here for five hundred years. It doesn't make any sense, but I get mad when I think about whoever is with her right now, whoever is explaining to her where she is and how she came to be here. Whoever it is who thinks they're about to spend eternity with her. Just the thought of that conversation happening right now makes my chest tight. I curl my hands into fists. *They're wrong.* I'm going to bring her back.

Which reminds me.

"Hey," I call over to Val, trying to keep my voice just low enough. We've been trying not to talk, but this is urgent. "Won't someone wonder where you are?"

He pushes a forefinger to his lips and motions for me to climb down. We both carefully step, squinting to see clearly in the moonlight, until we're both safely on the ground again.

"I don't have any friends here," he tells me finally. "They even gave me my own tent. Most of them share tents, and it's just a few of the tents that are really packed full. Most of the tents are empty."

"Do you think they'll have put Grace in an empty one too?" I ask, feeling hopeful.

"Nah. They'll try to win her over for a few days at least. That's what they tried to do with me, until I made it clear I wanted nothing to do with them. They were all acting like they'd done me a favor. They died so many years ago, and they think that what Gozzelino did to them was good: they never got to grow older, never got to get sick young and suffer a hard death like they'd seen so many of their family do. When Gozzelino stole all of their souls at once, he got so many years added to his weird life that he hasn't had to do it again until now."

"Why is he doing it this way, then? One at a time?"

Val doesn't say anything for a moment—he's silent long enough that I think maybe he fell asleep. But then he says, "Maybe he thinks he's close to getting his cure-all elixir right. He has been really happy lately."

I don't know what to make of that, but it doesn't make a lot of sense to me. If Gozzelino got all those years to work uninterrupted, why would he want to keep bringing the carnival back to get just one kid at a time?

"Why is there day and night here, anyway? Can't it just be day all the time?"

He shrugs. "Maybe they wanted a sense of normalcy. I really don't have all the answers, you know."

I know, but I don't like it. I want someone to know what they're doing; I want someone to absolve me of responsibility; I want a guide, or a parent, or even just a friend who is quicker than me. I want to sit around and make jokes while someone else does the real work. But what I said was true: nobody is coming to save me. I have to become the person I want to have in my life.

After an hour, we move in to find Grace. Val thinks she's probably in the biggest tent, the one next to Gozzelino's. Apparently Gozzelino lives and works in his own tent, the one at the head of the circle, but the one next to it is shorter, squatter, and more ragged, and that's where most of the kids stay. I'm still a little confused as to why ghosts sleep—Val insists it just makes them feel normal, and I guess that accounts for a lot. How many things do I do and say just out of habit? Do I ever really think about if the things I do and say actually make sense or are the best way to move forward, or do I just live my life out of habit?

But sleeping because it is comforting to them poses a challenge for us: since none of the children are actually sleeping—just pretending to sleep—we're going to have a harder time sneaking past them than if they were actually conked out for the night.

"Imagine you're in the car, on a road trip or something, and you just leaned your head against the seat and closed your eyes," explains Val. "You're resting. It feels nice, but at any moment, your mom could say something that would bring you out of it entirely. That's what sleeping is like to the dead. It's just a chance to rest, but there's no physical need to actually go to sleep."

"So you never dream?"

Val frowns. "Even if I do get my body back, I'd be happy if I never dreamed again. This week has been like living inside a nightmare."

We creep out of the forest together and near the tents. Val goes first into the circle to check that everything is clear, and then he motions for me to come closer. Here, I can get a better look at the carnival. It's set up much like I saw it in the square: little stages, discarded instruments propped up against the puppet theater, colorful bunting that looks muted in the moonlight. As terrifying as the prospect of spending eternity here without your family sounds, I can see why the kids who are already here have fun with it. The scene is whimsical and delightful, and if there's never a need to leave, I'm not sure why anyone would want to. The kids who are here already probably saw the adults in their lives, not much older than themselves, die horribly, from all kinds of diseases that we don't see anymore. Did Gozzelino believe he was saving them from all that? Val said he talked about his mom a lot—did he really just not want anyone else to die like her? Or is he trying to prove something to her, even in death?

Val enters the tent first while I wait outside. I listen hard at the entrance. The dim light radiating from my chest barely registers in the brightness of the moon, but I hold my hand over it to remind me that it's there. I'm still alive. I can do this.

When he locates Grace, the plan is for him to go to the opposite side of the tent and ask if anyone's got an extra pillow. I'm then to slip inside, walk over the children, rouse Grace, and leave with her. He'll join us in the morning.

The inside of the tent is so quiet for so long that I wonder if something's happened to him. It's not that long, probably only about sixty seconds, but to me, standing out in the circle of the night-time carnival, it feels like an eternity. Impulsively, I reach my hand out to open the entrance of the tent, but something—a little voice inside me—makes me stop. Death is inevitable, the gladiator had said, but Grace and Val deserve a chance to live before they die. They need me. I wait.

I feel a bit like a cat stalking its prey, with my head leaned forward and my eyes fixated on one diamond sewn onto the wall of the tent. Eventually, the question comes, like a lantern in the darkness, on the right side:

"Anyone got an extra pillow?"

Val's voice is neither loud nor too quiet, and there is no answer, but I do hear some shuffling around. Maybe they think he's finally coming around. Maybe they're annoyed with him for taking this long to join them. To be safe, though, I wait a little longer. I make myself count ten long, slow breaths, and then another ten. After the third set, I gradually reach my hand out, open the flap, and slip inside.

Terror like I've never known fills me as I see them all there, piled up on the ground like the dead they are. Each one looks solid, but shimmers in an unearthly way that lets me know this is no kindergarten naptime. Most of them are snuggled together with someone on their right or left, and it strikes me suddenly that this may have been how they slept when they were alive, with a parent or a sister or brother. They didn't have heat, after all, and they had to keep warm somehow. It's summer here, as it is back in the real world, and I wonder if this world also has seasons or is in a perpetual summer. I cannot stop to ponder that, though—I look to my left and see Grace immediately, sleeping on her own with a little patchwork quilt covering her. I am grateful to whoever covered her, whether she really needed it or not. It seems like a small kindness.

Gingerly, I step over one kid and another, my breath frozen in my throat and my heart pounding. Just as I am about to reach Grace, someone grabs my ankle.

I want to scream, but I suppress the urge. Instead, I cross my arms tighter over my chest and wait. The light at my heart is probably still visible, but it makes me feel better to cover it. Just in case.

"What, friend?" says a small voice. "The sun still hides, come and rest."

My throat is dry, but I force myself to answer. "Yes, thank you."

The ghost holds my hand and pulls me down. I lie down on the ground beside her, covering my heart with my other hand. I stare up at the ceiling of the tent. I count my breaths.

Slowly, I turn my head to look at this child who pulled me down. A little girl with her eyes closed. She has a bluish cast but otherwise looks like a girl a few grades below me at a costume party. I put my feet on the ground and feel the earth under my feet. *This is real,* I tell myself. *These are my real feet. This is the real earth.* Which may be true or untrue, but it's something I need to hear.

I get up; I creep toward Grace again. This time, I reach her.

I realize that I never formulated a plan for how to wake her up. With my free hand, I touch her shoulder.

She opens her eyes and looks at me with an expression I've never seen before, on anyone. A mixture of terror and hope, joy and horror together, both so fully present in her eyes. I put a finger to my lips, and she nods vigorously.

I motion for her to follow me, and then I have to trust that she is as I step over the sleeping children. When I get out of the tent, it feels like I've arrived on land after swimming for my life. Grace follows me.

"I knew you'd come," says Grace. "I don't know why, but I knew I'd see you again."

I take her hand, and we run behind the puppet stage. I don't know why, but what she said makes me feel actually brave, not the fake brave that I've pretended to be my whole life. She depended on me. She knew I'd come for her. She had faith in me.

And I actually came through.

I'm as surprised as anyone.

18

A few minutes pass, and Val joins us. As we run toward the grave together, I keep thinking, *I can't believe we actually pulled it off. I can't believe we actually did it.* Soon, all of us will be on the other side, and this will all seem like it was a bad dream.

We intuitively slow as we get closer. I don't want to accidentally get too close and trip, and besides, I don't know what the process of jumping through the grave is actually going it be like. Will it be like falling a longer way? Will it be night when we arrive back home? How will I get Val and Grace back to their bodies? How will they get back inside them?

When we finally do reach the empty grave, I sense they have the same questions because we all hesitate. "You first," I tell Val.

"Um...okay."

He jumps in. But he doesn't go anywhere; he just lands down in the hole in the ground like it's an ordinary pit.

"Maybe it only works if you do it," he tells me from below. "Help me up, and then you go down."

"What if I make it back and you two don't?"

"We'll keep trying," says Grace. "You go. And if we don't make it..."

"You need to make it," I say, gritting my teeth. "Otherwise this whole plan was for nothing."

"Mia," says Val. It's the first time he's said my name, and the way he says it makes me feel like he's an adult telling a toddler that they really have to go to bed now. "We'll go in right after you, okay? But just in case... remember your promise."

"I am not about to go off by myself and tell the police I just got back from a mystical carnival filled with dead children and now know where two bodies are stashed. I'm not doing that."

"Yes, you are. You promised."

"I know what I promised." I'm sweating now, and I feel feverish. I glance down at the light in my chest and notice it's flickering now. "We'll jump in together. Hold my hands. We'll go side by side."

Grace moves to my right and Val to my left, and I grip their icy hands, and we all bring our toes closer to the edge. "Okay," I say. "Let's hope this works."

"If it doesn't..."

"I know, Val! A long night of interrogation at the police station for me. Don't remind me." The fact that I'm still making dumb jokes right now is just sad, but I don't know what else to do. I don't have another way out of this. "One."

Val's grip tightens on my left. "Two."

Grace nods her head resolutely. "Three."

We jump.

We land in the dirt, still at the Bone Carnival. I want to scream. Instead, I release their hands and pound both fists into the dirt wall in front of me, loosening a few clumps, which fall to our feet.

"Oh," says a voice above us. "Is your fun finished?"

The silhouette of a cat's head against the full silver moon is above us. In just a few slow seconds, he transforms into a man again—Gozzelino.

"I'm afraid this is more of a long-term commitment than a fleeting entertainment," he says in a silky voice. He's speaking to all of us, I think, but his eyes land on me. "And I see one of you has yet to commit."

I scowl. "None of us have committed to anything. You stole them!"

"I am no thief. I very reasonably explained what we were all doing here, then asked for a volunteer. It is not my fault if the weight of the consequences are not understood."

I try to keep my chin from quivering, but it's an uphill battle. "I was the one who volunteered, not Grace."

"A useful lesson, if you'll take it," says Gozzelino, smiling. "Lie with dogs and expect fleas. Though I'm lucky to have gotten the dog as well. Then again," he stretches out his fingers toward the light in my chest, "I've always been lucky."

There's a force around me now, and it raises me into the air. I feel the pull on my heart first, and then my feet leave the earth. Soon, I'm hovering several feet above the grave, unable to move. I want to wiggle out of this and jump free onto the ground, but whatever he's doing is preventing me from moving my body at all. Grace and Val watch in horror below.

"Val," says Gozzelino, his hand still raised to keep me in the air, "Grace. Will you two please go and wake the others? We have another ceremony to perform."

"No," says Val, but I hear the rattle in his voice as well. "You can't do anything to us."

"Can't I?" asks Gozzelino. "Does it occur to you that there might be places far worse than this, where some of the dead go, where you might find yourselves if you do not comply? I plucked this carnival from life and used magic to make it last forever. The residents here appreciate what I have done for them. But what if I hadn't? Do you really want to find out where naughty boys and girls go when they die?"

Val is silent. After a moment, I hear Grace's voice, and it has no tremble at all:

"You don't scare us."

"Then you are fools. And this is no place for fools. I will drain this girl's life," he flickers his eyes at me, "and then I will show you what happens to the ungrateful. Franco!"

The wall of the tent ripples and out steps the biggest boy, the one who had carried Grace to the center of the circle. In no time at all, he is at Gozzelino's side, leering up at me. His teeth are black and misshapen, and he looks as if he's just waiting for permission to rip us apart.

"Franco, take these two," he gestures into the grave, where Val and Grace stand defiant but cornered, "back to camp. I'll take care of their friend."

Franco reaches into the grave and picks them both up by their collars like a pair of baby cats, and then he marches them both toward the carnival. Gozzelino waves his hand lazily to one side, and it's like a gust from a tornado rushes onto my right side. I am flung to the left. I hit the ground and bounce. My mouth suddenly tastes like blood.

"Get up," he snarls. I do, but only to show him that he hasn't won. I can still stand. I make myself look at his face.

After our eyes stay locked for a few seconds, he smiles. "You think you're being brave by fighting to keep your life your own," he says. "Come with me, and I'll show you what true bravery is."

19

He walks me back into the carnival, which is in full swing once again. The sun is just rising, but underneath the pink-and-purple cotton candy sky, the band is playing, the jugglers and acrobats are warming up, and every face we pass laughs at me as I go by. Eventually, we get to Gozzelino's tent: a smaller but heavy-looking red-and-gold dwelling, speckled with stars and moons that seem to twinkle as we get nearer. He holds the flap open and makes a polite gesture for me to come in too. Since I have no choice in the matter, I do.

I gasp when I step inside. I expected it to look just like the tent that all the kids were sleeping in earlier, but instead, it's like we're immediately transported to somewhere else entirely; we're in a sort of dungeon with stone walls and a large kitchen. A fireplace is straight ahead with an iron caldron over a roaring fire, bubbling and boiling. Glass jars and vials with brightly colored liquids line the walls on wooden shelves.

"I make sure to show all the children this room so they know what a noble sacrifice they're making." He gestures to an armchair that matches the outside of the tent—the red material has gold and silver stars on it as well. "Sit down, sit down! You see, Mia, I am not the evil villain you might imagine me to be."

He waits, smiling at me, until I sit. He sits in a matching chair across from me and continues: "You just have something I need in order to do some good in the world, you see. I've been working on this potion for a long time. My mother and grandfather both died, and though the illness they died from just causes a minor inconvenience to the affected now, there are so many more that could be cured. Imagine it, Mia. A world free from disease. Free from sickness. Everyone on earth could live their best lives, for as long as they wanted, and then drop dead one day from old age, happy and free. Don't you want that for everyone?"

I don't respond. It does sound pretty good.

"Capturing the entire carnival I saw outside my window that day, I was sure, was a mercy for everyone there. Instead of living pitifully short lives and dying of some horrid disease, suffering for a long time, they could be part of the solution for all mankind. I could take their remaining years to restore some of my power—it took a lot to bring all of us here, after all, in an unused realm between life and death—and they could be happy forever, enjoying a carefree afterlife."

"So why come back?" I ask, suppressing a shiver, despite the roaring fire in the hearth. "You took all these years from all these people. Why take more?"

He frowns. "As you might guess, it wasn't enough. I am almost finished with this potion. It is almost done. Another five to eight hundred years—oh, maybe a thousand—would do it."

"What?" I ask, confused now. That's nowhere near almost done, and even taking all three of us wouldn't give him another one thousand years.

"Yes," he says. "Gathering that many years from a large group of children is going to take quite a bit of power. I simply needed the life forces from one or two children in order to gather the power I needed for that."

"So then..." I say slowly, wishing I were smarter, wishing I were quicker and more calculating, like Grace. But it's not Grace here—it's me, and I have to do this. "You're not taking our lives to get the rest of the years you need to finish this elixir."

"No, stupid girl, didn't I just say that?" he spits out the words like he's disgusted with me. He jumps up from the chair and paces on the red rug underneath us. "Your years, and those of your two friends outside, are going to be used for me to capture something larger. I would have only needed another one if you hadn't forced me to control those stupid tourists in the grave-yard. But I'm recovered now, and I only need some more time to finish this. More children. Luckily, as I observed in my feline form, the world has changed quite a bit."

I shift in my seat, eyeing the door. It's a large wooden one, and it's almost unbelievable to think that the other side looks like the flap of a tent, even though I saw it myself. He laughs.

"You look as though you're getting ready to run."

143

"Where would I run?" I ask, my voice cold.

"Exactly. So," he crosses one ankle over a knee and clasps his hands on it, "the world has changed, in some big ways and some small ones. One way that hasn't changed at all is how some parents feel about their children. I'll share with you that my mother felt the same about me as yours feels about you. Does that make sense to you?"

My body turns to stone. I have never talked to anyone except Enzo about how I think Mom feels about me.

"My mother," he continues, "was not ambitious, like yours, but she had a carefree life, and she liked it that way. Her easy magic gave her everything she could ever want, and so when she wanted a child, she got one of those too. Me. She liked being seen as a mother, but only when it suited her. When it didn't, which was most of the time, I was left in the care of nannies, who beat me and berated me and told me children should be seen and not heard. I always told myself that one day, I'd prove to my mother that I was worth much more than she valued me, but she ruined things by dying too early. Do you think that stopped me? No." He grinned with a show-biz grade smile. "Not all afterlives are the same. If she is able to see the earth from wherever she is now, she will soon know what her son has done for the entire world." He uncrosses his legs and takes a little green glass vial from the shelf.

"What's this?"

"Just orange seed oil. Take a whiff. You look a little pale."

I do not move, and so he says, "Oh, for heaven's sake," uncorks it, and holds it under his own nose. "You see? Harmless."

I take it, but I don't hold it as close to my face as he did. It smells horrible anyway.

"So you see, we are alike. I thought you'd respect what we were doing here, and so I came to you."

"We are nothing alike."

"No?" He lifts his brows. "You don't have anything you want to prove to your mother?"

I open my mouth, and then close it again. Sure, I sometimes get the feeling she looks at me the way you'd look at a dog that has rolled in something smelly, but she's still my mom. I'm still going to get back to her. Aren't I?

He sighs at my silence. "It isn't just you and I. Now, anybody who has a baby can give them to nurses, who put them all into brightly-colored rooms all day and pick them up one by one. Daycare, they call it now. I can simply take one or two of those rooms, and I'll have as many years as I need."

"Babies?" My jaw drops and my stomach flips, but he just crinkles his nose.

"Yes, but we won't keep their souls here, obviously. Imagine all the crying. No fun at all. But it's perfect, since babies don't know anything anyway. Probably don't even feel pain. As such, I have the perfect place for them, which is what I wanted to show you in the first place. Come here."

He reaches for a small leather-bound book the size of a diary and opens it. The aged yellow pages have pictures on them, and on more careful observation, the pictures are moving. His pointed finger lands on a full-page picture of a hell scene—demons are dancing around a fire with their sharp teeth bared and their claws outstretched. They see me staring at them from above and hiss at me.

"So what?" I say, embarrassed immediately that my voice is a squeak. "Am I supposed to be scared of a little book?"

"Let's see." He reaches for the shelf beside him and takes a jar of black-winged beetles. He uncrews the jar, and they scurry to avoid his hand when he reaches in and grabs one. The unlucky beetle flails in his calm hand. He tosses the insect into the picture, and as soon as it hits the page, it becomes an ink drawing, just like the demons. They engulf it, ripping off its wings and antennae, stomping its body beneath their clawed feet. Even though I don't want him to know how afraid I am, I gasp.

"Despite what they preach in the churches and teach in the storybooks, there are many ways to be dead, and many places you can spend your afterlife," Gozzelino says cooly, screwing the lid back on the jar and placing it back onto the shelf. "You can suffer, forever, the way our little insect friend will now. You can haunt a favorite place, or even an object, in the world of the living, without being seen or heard by them. Or you can be here, at a carnival, having fun with your friends for all eternity.

"I'll give you and your friends one more chance. You may stay here, make friends with the others, and enjoy your afterlife, or," he gestures to the book again, where the horned demons are now reaching out their arms, begging Gozzelino for another plaything, "I can send you there. Very easily. Understood?"

I nod.

This is going to be harder than I thought, but I'm not going to give up. Even if he takes my years, they still exist. They still exist.

But it looks as if my theory is about to be put to the test. He takes a dirty rag and a vial of clear liquid and coats it.

"This next part is unpleasant, I'm afraid. But as you've seen, I am merciful." He holds the rag to my nose, and my vision blurs. Soon the shelves swirl, the ceiling spins, and I am vaguely aware of dropping to the floor before everything turns to black.

20

I don't wake up until the next night. I feel a tugging at my legs, like my thighs are coming loose from my hips. I curl up to see what's happening. Two girls are dragging me toward the big tent. I try to ask them what they're doing, but only a tired-sounding groan comes out.

"Oh, hello," the older-looking one says. The smaller one, a girl of about five who has her same thick eyebrows, smiles kindly at me "It's time to rest."

"You can stay with us!" says the little one. "We've been longing for new friends for so long."

"Uh," I say, bringing myself up to sitting. "I don't feel well."

The older girl giggles. "Of course you don't feel well. You're dead now!"

I gulp and slowly look down at my chest. Yes, the dim light is gone. My skin is glowing blue, and I feel a strange cold feeling, like I'm inside a cool shadow in the wintertime.

"It takes a little time to get used to being dead," explains the girl, while her sister plays with my shoelace, twirling it around her finger. "We'll help you inside if you like. Or do you think you can walk?"

"I think," I say slowly, "I need more time."

Now the little girl laughs. "Time! That's what you paid for admission to the carnival!"

The bigger girl chuckles. "Can't get that back. But you'd like to be left alone, is that it?"

I nod. I want to find Val and Grace, but now I'm a little confused as well. They're not as bad as Val said. They don't deserve to be here, either. They were tricked too.

"Can you tell me where Grace and Val are?" I ask.

They both wrinkle their noses and give each other a look. Then the older one says, "They're not very nice, are they? The others don't like them at all. Are you sure you don't want to come into our tent with us? Be our friend?"

They sound so sincere that I want to say yes, because I know what it feels like to be so lonely. But we're running out of time: if Gozzelino wants to return to the world to lure a nursery full of babies to feed to the demons in his book, we have to stop him. Plus, I don't know how much longer Val has to return to his body. And then there's mine...

I look at the horizon and see Franco, the burly boy who does Gozzelino's dirty work, drag two people toward the grave we all tried to escape in the night before. Who are they? I try to get closer to have a look, but I'm still weak from whatever he's done to me.

But the two figures look so familiar, and even though I couldn't help if I tried, I still crawl, slowly, toward him to get a better look. I gasp when I recognize what I'm seeing—the swath of sandy-brown hair, the bony elbows, the pink sweatshirt...that's me. That's my body.

He tosses one into the grave first, which I can see now is Grace's, and then mine.

"No," I say weakly, stretching out an arm but lacking the strength to do anything more. "No."

And then I cry. What I want more than anything else in the world right now is for my parents to swoop in and punish me. I want them to tell me I'm lucky nobody got hurt, that I should be grateful all I'm getting is a grounding and not something far worse—I had no idea what they were talking about, but I do now. I wish, I wish, I wish.

"Mia?"

Grace softly sits down beside me. "I'm sorry, Mia."

Val sits on the other side, not speaking.

"I'm sorry too." I'm speaking to both of them, and I mean it. I'm sorry for not being able to save Grace. I'm sorry for not going back to tell Val's mom where his body was. I'm sorry I'm not smarter, faster, better. I'm sorry I'm me.

"Gozzelino says you willingly sacrificed yourself?" asks Val bitterly. "He says you understood this was for the good of humanity. How could you?"

I shake my head, still deep in sadness.

"Is that what you think, Mia?"

Grace puts her arm around me. "Shut up, Val."

Val does not shut up. "I want to know. Are you really stupid enough to believe he wants to save the world?"

Grace scowls at him, but I finally find my voice again. It's quiet, and its scratchy, but it's mine. "He lied to you. I didn't willingly sacrifice myself."

This takes Val aback for a moment, and he is quiet.

"That's what I told him," Grace snaps. "But Mia—we still have a chance. All of us. He's a little stronger now that he has your years, but he's still too weak to keep working on his elixir. If we could find the bone and then reconnect it to his finger, we might be able to leave this place."

I notice her words—not "get back home," but "leave this place." There are many ways to die, Gozzelino says. Many places to go. It's true the next world might not be as pleasant as this one could be, but she's right. Even if it's too late to save ourselves, we can still stop Gozzelino from cutting more lives short.

"Oh, sure," Val scoffs beside us. "Find the bone. I'm sure it's just playing peek-a-boo. We'll find it under a couch cushion or something."

Franco is walking toward us now after disposing of Grace's body and mine. I expect him to scowl at us or something, but instead, he keeps his eyes down, looking almost embarrassed. I cock my head to the side as I watch him rejoin a group of children. They're kicking a ball back and forth, like soccer. He starts to smile, and looks over at us, but only just for an instant.

I think back on the girls who were trying to drag me around. *We've been longing for new friends for so long,* they'd said.

Maybe it was time for them to get their wish.

"I really am sorry, Val. I want your mom to know where your body is, and I want mine and Grace's to know too. But Grace is right: we can still stop Gozzelino," I say, "we might just need a bit of help."

21

Val still thinks it's stupid, but Grace and I go over to the group with Franco. The laughing and shouting quiets gradually as we get closer; the last kids to stop turn around to gawk at us as we approach.

"Can we play?"

No one says a word. For a second, I think maybe something is wrong, maybe they're angry at us for trying to escape. But after a few seconds of uncomfortable silence, Franco himself kicks the ball over to us. I dribble between my feet a few times and then kick it over to Grace. She has obviously never played soccer before, because she kind of nudges it with her toe before stepping forward and kicking it properly toward me again. I use the inside of my foot to kick it back to Franco, who gives me a smile. I return it.

We keep playing like that, not playing a real game, just kind of passing it back and forth, until some music starts up in the main circle, and some of the kids go to hear them play. Franco hangs back and walks beside me.

"I'm sorry about the..." he says, putting a hand to the back of his neck. "You know. I hope your parents find your bodies soon. I'm sure they will."

"Thanks," I say, trying my best to keep things casual even though I want to scream, to shake him, to kick and stomp and writhe at the urgency of the situation. Among my own team back in Louisville, I am infamous for having absolutely no chill. Is this progress, then? "Did your parents ever find yours?"

"Huh?" he asks, and I realize it's possible that he could have forgotten them. Just as I'm scolding myself for asking such a dumb question, he clears his throat. "Oh, my mom and dad had died before the carnival got taken. Most of us had been taken in by the church. They took us to the carnival one day; Gozzelino asked if if we'd like to stay, and we said yes. Gozzelino brought us here, and I'm not even sure anyone noticed. The sisters might have prayed for our souls, but I think they were happy we'd gone, all said and done."

"Oh."

"And we were. This place beats that drafty old convent. No beds, hard work, punishments every day, for little accidents, even! Things you didn't mean. Yes, this is better."

I'm trying to listen to him, but I can't help wondering what I'm going to say if he asks me how I like it here. I can lie convincingly, but I don't want to. Not about this. He doesn't, though, and the two of us settle down beside each other on the soft grass to watch a group of girls dance with ribbons tied on the ends of batons. The ribbons make almost-too-graceful circles in the air, like the laws of gravity are just a little looser here. Maybe they are.

I lean back on my palms. "So," I say, starting toward him again. "You never get bored of this?"

"I didn't say that. I just said this was better than the orphanage."

"You're bored, then?"

He laughs a little. "I think we all are. Wouldn't you be?" He frowns and looks away. "I'm sorry. I shouldn't have said it like that. After all, you'll know in another five hundred years."

"What if Gozzelino finishes his elixir before then? What happens to us then?"

A strange look crosses his face now: he's still smiling, but it's like he knows something. "Will he finish the elixir? Or is he afraid? These are things we wonder. Yet, if he does finish, all will be glorious. We will go...on."

How do normal people do this? *Chill,* I remind myself. *Play it cool.* "What's 'on?'"

He pinches his features together for a second and then says, "Nobody knows, exactly. But it's the place we're supposed to be. Maybe it's the place the nuns were trying to get to. Maybe it's just nothing. But whatever it is, I think it'll be a welcome change from the Bone Carnival."

Bingo. Not only does Franco not believe Gozzelino wants to do it, but he wants to leave this place. We might be able to trust them and work together. It's just like Dad said—instead of clinging to our roles as outsiders who save the day, Grace, Val, and I need to immerse ourselves. We need to listen to these kids and team up. They know a lot more than us.

I'm a little bit afraid I'll scare him off with questions, so I choose the next one carefully.

"What makes you think he's afraid? Is he afraid of the unknown?" My voice is too high, like a little girl's, so I clear my throat like it was just phlegm. Then I remember: I can't have phlegm without a body.

But Franco doesn't make fun of me; he shakes his head, then turns back, as if he doesn't want to be overheard. "Of seeing his family again."

Before I can ask what that's supposed to mean, someone else comes over and says they need one more for their team, and he jumps up without hesitation, like he's embarrassed to be seen with me.

"See ya," I say to his back.

The bare trees in the distance look like charcoal sketches against the gray sky. A question bubbles to the surface of my mind: If the kids, who outnumber Gozzelino fifty to one, want to move on from this world, why haven't they done it already?

It feels a little wrong to be in our separate tent, like we're dividing ourselves into cliques based on what century Gozzelino murdered us in.

"I still can't believe I'm actually dead," says Grace. "I thought it would feel different than this."

"What did you think it would feel like?" Val asks. I feel like I already know what Grace means just looking at Val—he's pulled off one of his socks and is trying to fix the hole in the toe. He opens his mouth slightly and squeezes one eye shut trying to thread the ancient-looking needle. I didn't know what the afterlife would look like, either, but I didn't imagine we'd still have holes in our socks.

"I don't think I ever thought about it, really. Maybe I thought when we died, we just died. It was over. Just the idea of being in one place for even five hundred years...it's almost too much. But when I think of being here for *all of eternity,* it's like my brain is going to explode."

"We are not going to be here for all of eternity," I say. "Listen."

I tell them what Franco told me about moving on, and that they didn't believe that Gozzelino actually could or wanted to finish his elixir. He just couldn't let the job go, for some reason. Val is a terrible listener and keeps asking me what I mean (though, to be fair, I also asked Franco about what "on" meant—I guess some unknowns are always uncomfortable) but Grace looks at me with that intense, focused look on her face and tells Val to shut up and let me talk until I'm done.

"But it doesn't make any sense," Val groans. "You say that the ghosts in the Colosseum told you just to put the severed bone back on his finger and his dark magic would be reversed. If it's so easy, why hasn't anyone done it?"

"I think," I say, the swirling thoughts in my head just now forming themselves into words, "they're scared. Franco says most of them came from an orphanage. They know that as long as they're here, and the elixir isn't done yet, they're safe."

"So you're sure it has nothing to do with wanting to save all of humanity from every possible disease?" Grace asks.

"I don't think so."

"So we won't have to turn them against Gozzelino." Grace purses her lips and nods, as if trying to convince herself. "And if we pull this off, we may get to go back to our bodies and our lives."

"And if we're wrong?" asks Val.

"We'll just go where they go," I say. "On."

22

There's a lot of things I'd do if I weren't dead.

I'd probably get to know these kids better. I'd ask them a billion questions about what life was like before iPads and airplanes and indoor plumbing. I'd tell them about the golden age of television and how even though the sitcoms were great back then, they're even greater now because we can watch them whenever we want, not just, like, Thursdays at eight o'clock. I'd get Grace to organize secret meetings; I'd listen to what everyone had to say, and we'd help each other get out of the Bone Carnival and onto—well, just on—together.

But even though we're fully dead now, I can't shake the feeling that, if we can act fast to extinguish Gozzelino's magic, we could still get back to our bodies. Val doesn't think so, but I do. We have a book at our home of all the different ways there are to die, and though a lot of them are just plain grue-some—brain-eating amoebas, stuck by lightning, blunt trauma (which really just means getting clunked really

hard on the head with something heavy)—the intro-
duction of the book begins by saying just how wired
the human body is to survive. People have survived
horrible events, owing no credit to themselves at all—
it's just the body's amazing ability to just keep going.
We're not as fragile as we believe we are, the author
says. People have even been legally pronounced dead
and have come back, but when I tell this to Val, he
says that's just in the hospital, when somebody's heart
stops beating for a few minutes.

Still! I know it's not impossible. I just know it.

Or maybe I just hope it.

Grace comes back and confirms that Gozzelino is
still in the square, dancing and listening to the music
and definitely not in the tent working on the elixir he
claims is the entire point of being here. She says Val
will be able to get into his tent if the two of us can
capture his interest long enough. Val's almost done
with his needle and thread, this time sewing a tiny
purple robe and yellow crown, which we'll place on
the Gozzelino marionette. Our plan is set.

"Ready?" I say, but I'm almost out of the tent already.
"Mia?"

I turn around. Val and Grace stand there with their
arms at their sides, looking like someone buried their
feet in the sand.

"What's wrong?" I ask them.

"Aren't you afraid?" Grace says, almost whispering.
"Should we talk it over some more? What if this
doesn't work?"

"He's already killed us," says Val. "What if he opens
that book again and...and..."

He swallows so hard I can see his throat contract and expand again. I step toward them both. Even though I am all spirit now, I still feel fear the same way I'd feel it in my body. Hot everywhere except my ice-cold hands, which are shaking. Dry eyes. Light headed and disoriented. Even my loose tooth feels the same, forever just hanging on, but making me sick to my stomach, just as if I were alive. As I look at them, I can tell they're feeling it in their afterlife bodies too.

"My dad says the things I do are shenanigans, but I've always been daring. I always thought I could just work with fear, make it my friend, but the truth is I never did anything that mattered much. This matters. Giving those kids a chance at real happiness matters. Making Gozzelino face justice matters. And getting back to our real lives, where we can make our own choices, matters. But I know what you're feeling right now—it's fear. I feel it too. It's going to help us be quicker and sharper and more observant and more cautious when that counts. We know what we need to do now. We need to all make a pact with ourselves to just do it, and we'll be over the hardest part."

Grace lifts her head and gives me a quick nod, keeping her eyes on mine. Val stands there, stone-faced.

"We need you, Val," I tell him. "We need to come together to do this."

"Like a family," he murmurs. "Families come together when hard things need to be done."

The word *family* takes me aback, makes me draw a breath. Not a real breath, of course—but something like it.

"Like a family," Grace confirms for me, nodding her head.

"A family," I say, feeling a little steadier on my feet. "But one we choose ourselves. Now, is your needle threaded?"

"Yes."

I turn to Grace. "Know what you're going to say?"

Grace nods again.

"Good. Now just tell yourself, 'I am going to walk out of this tent.' Walking out will be the hardest part, and after that, it'll all be easy. The fear will help."

"Maybe we should call it anticipation," says Grace.

"Yes, good. I like that," I say. Maybe this is why none of the other kids tried this before—I've had years of practice in dealing with anticipation, as Grace calls it. I know the first step is the hardest.

I draw a breath for courage and hastily pull the little purple robe onto the Gozzelino puppet. Val takes one of his needles and sews around the strings, so the puppet is fully dressed. Grace crowns it, and Val adds a quick stitch to his hair as well to keep the crown on. We need the real Gozzelino to see that crown, so we can't take a chance of it falling off, not even for a moment. Enzo would call that a bad omen.

Thinking about Enzo makes the corners of my mouth dip. I don't want to leave him alone with Mom and Dad.

"Okay," says Val when the thread is knotted and cut. "First step, here we go."

We step out of the tent. Val goes on ahead, but Grace and I move to the little puppet stage. I make

Gozzelino prance around on his strings while Grace alternates between adoring sighs and applause.

It isn't long before the real Gozzelino sees what we're doing. He comes over and expresses delight over the little robe and crown.

"What is this?" he says. "You've given me a new costume!"

I smile broadly, all my best practice at lying to adults finally paying off. "Do you like it?"

"Very much! Come on, tell me about this. You want to have a masquerade ball, is that it? One where we all dress up and dance all night?" He claps his hands together. "Marvelous idea. We'll have one tonight."

"Perfect!" I say, the cheeriness in my voice bubbling over, "we were just talking about how we'll all be remembered once the elixir is done. Once everyone on Earth knows what it took to make it, they'll think of you as a king, and they'll have festivals in our honor. Maybe even just like this!"

His shining eyes move from me to the puppet. "Yes," he says. "It will happen, you know. I was always destined for greatness! You haven't gone nearly far enough with this little costume, but it's the right idea, and I'm glad you're coming around to reality. They will erect statues in my honor, buildings, a city, even, named after me. You'll see."

"Do you want to see what I imagine? I can tell you the story with the theater."

Gozzelino's bright eyes flash with delight. He motions to three kids standing next to him, and they start getting the puppet theater ready—tying back the curtains, shuffling set pieces inside. Grace drops the puppet down while I tell the story. When everyone turns their backs to Val to watch the show, I sneeze—the signal to Val. From the corner of my eye, I see him disappear into Gozzelino's tent. Cold prickles burst at my forehead as I wait for someone to follow him, but no one does.

I begin.

"The day the great Gozzelino finishes his elixir, he goes first to Italy's best scientists. They thank him and spend the next few years proving that it works to cure every imaginable disease. It seems almost impossible, but they confirm it, and soon the entire world is full of wonder. Possibilities are open to people who had no hope. What is everyone going to do with their long and healthy life? So many possibilities, so many different paths, but while everyone is thinking their own opportunities over, they all fall to their knees at least once a day and thank Gozzelino!"

I look over their heads. The coast is still clear. *Just be patient. Trust Val,* I tell myself. I slip back into the crowd while Grace takes up the story from here.

Grace speaks in her soothing, melodic tone, Gozzelino and the others hanging on her every word. "Italy is the world's superpower again, of course, and Rome, as Gozzelino's home city, has become the capital of the world. Gozzelino has enough power to stay in the world and walk among the living for the rest of his days, thanks to the combination of his magic and the elixir. They crown him king, and he has the most power any human in history has ever had. He is rich beyond all imagination. He is universally loved."

I check over my shoulder. I'm getting nervous now. Where is Val?

"People travel to Rome from around the globe to thank him for their long lives. There's not a child in the world who doesn't know his name. Songs are written about him, great works of art are commissioned. He decides to go on only when he wants to, after he's had a long and happy enjoyment of the fruits of his labor."

From the audience, on cue, I turn from the puppet Gozzelino to the real one. "When are you going to do it? Will we be able to see all this?" It makes me sick to see his expression, calm and content and almost dreamy. I know what it's like to get lost in your own daydreams, and I also know what it's like to have them be so strong they drive you to act.

"Don't worry, child, I will not let them forget you. I'll need a few more lives, but if you like, I can use some of the magic to allow you to see what your sacrifice has meant to the world."

"But when?" asks the older girl I met earlier. She looks eager, but I doubt it's to see the world worship Gozzelino.

I stand up and slowly back up toward the tent. Grace flashes me a look of concern.

"Yes, when?" asks her older sister.

When I reach Gozzelino's tent, I claw like a hungry cat until I get it open. I don't think anyone sees me.

I hope.

Val is on all fours. He looks so scared when he sees me.

"Mia!"

165

"Oh, no." I drop down beside him. "Please don't tell me—"

"I lost the needle," he says miserably. "I dropped it somewhere over here."

I start patting the ground, but that's getting us nowhere fast. I stand and start looking through Gozzelino's things instead.

"What are you doing?" Val asks. "Help me find it!"

But I've already found what I need. I knew I'd find one around here somewhere. Gozzelino may be a sorcerer, but it looks like he still has a soft spot for simple magic tricks, too. I hold up the large magnet.

"Mia," Val whispers. "What we *need* is a—"

I do a quick sweep of the ground and instantly the magnet finds the needle. Metal meets metal with a little *click*.

"Oh," says Val.

I hand him the glove, and he gets to work, sewing the bone into one of the fingers. I start to go outside, but something catches my eye—the little demon book Gozzelino used to threaten me. I take it now and slip it under the elastic waistband of my shorts, just in case.

Outside, we can hear the entire crowd of children anxiously asking Gozzelino:

"This year?"

"This month?"

"When?"

"When?"

"When?"

"Now, children," he says, and his tone betrays his nervousness, "these things do take time."

"But you'll be king of the world! And you won't have to sulk around the world as a cat anymore; you can stride around as the most beloved man who ever lived!" I say. I can't have him getting cold feet now; he has to be inspired. He has to act. Now. "Think of your mother!"

I feel a wave of realization go through the crowd of kids. Several look at me with wide eyes, but the rest claw at Gozzelino. The energy among us soars.

The little girl clasps her hands together, sending the braid under her little cap flying backward. "Your mother will be so proud!"

"Get the children!"

"Go!"

"Please!"

Val comes out of the tent, holding Gozzelino's boots and gloves. There's a little loose thread on one of the fingers, but I hope Gozzelino is too eager to go back to Rome to notice.

"Ha!" says Gozzelino, taking his boots, "so eager to see your legacy come to life. I can understand that. Yes of course, I can. All right, then. Thank you, Franco." Franco helps him get into his boots. Behind him, Val fiddles with the gloves nervously.

I try with all my might to communicate with the two of them. *Val, stop acting like the most frightened kindergartner on the first day of school. Franco, please, please be on our side.*

Gozzelino is still talking as Franco takes the first glove from Val and hands it to his master. "There's not much left to it all, to tell the truth. Just a few more lives to gather, and then the elixir will be done, and we will all be immortalized in the minds of all generations to come. All of us."

As he brags, I watch Val and Franco carefully. Franco takes the last glove and frowns. I watch as he pinches one of the fingers of the glove and feels the bone inside. The bottom drops out of my stomach. *Please,* I say, though I do not know who I am talking to exactly. *Please.*

But Val locks eyes with Franco, and silently the two communicate, though I can't quite tell what they're saying to each other. It's a move I know—my brother and I do it every now and then, when our parents make excuses to leave for errands or work on weekends or eat dinner in their offices instead of with us. It's a way for us to see the silent, shared scar on each other. It's a way to remind each other that we aren't alone.

I hope that's what's happening with Franco and Val, anyway.

"Franco, please," Gozzelino says, "I must have both my gloves." He starts to turn toward the two boys.

Before he can look at Franco, I burst out, "Three cheers for king Gozzelino!" I'm nearly screaming. "Hip, hip!"

"Hooray!"

Franco takes the glove and turns to the smugly smiling Gozzelino.

"Hip, hip!"

"Hooray!"

Gozzelino holds out his hand. Franco, holding open the glove with the severed bone sewed into the last finger, takes a deep breath as Gozzelino slides his hand inside.

"Hip, hip!"

There is no last cheer. With Gozzelino's hand inside the glove, the bone touches his body.

The whole is restored. He feels it, too. He tries to take his hand out of the glove, but it won't come off.

"No," he says, tearing at it. "No! You little devils!"

I gulp, feeling the demon book pressing against my hip under my clothes. But something's off—his skeleton is back together, and the unnatural magic shouldn't be keeping us here anymore.

But for some reason, we remain.

23

When Gozzelino finally realizes he can't take off the glove, he curls his spine down toward the ground and lets out a mighty roar. And then he lifts his eyes to me, ablaze with anger.

"You," he says.

I think for a second he's going to run at me, but instead he sweeps back, nearly flying into his tent. I can guess what he's looking for, and it's hidden under my clothes.

"Look!" Grace says and points to my chest.

It's glowing.

The yellowish-green light is an orb that floats just inside my chest. When I reach my fingers up, I see that it responds to my touch—I can take it out and put it back in, kind of like a balloon filled with just enough helium to gently hover in the air.

I look around then to see that everyone has a glow now. Grace's is lavender-colored and medium-sized; Franco's is the color of a dreamsicle and much larger. Val cups his inside his hands, a sage ball of light.

"Our lives," he whispers.

We're in charge of our own time again. Mine feels delicate, buoyant, and vibrant, like a water lily on a pond. I'm in awe of it, but I'm also confused. If it's mine again, why am I still here?

A second roar makes the whole world vibrate with fury. Gozzelino bursts out of the tent and points a finger at me. "I will find it!" he screams. "I will find it, and I will feed your soul to the demons!"

"You can't," says Franco quietly.

Gozzelino's face stiffens, as if he knows it's true.

"Who will be my brave volunteer?"

"Did he come to your window? Did you follow him into the carnival?"

"He asked us to come, and we said yes."

"He's only in charge of our lives if let him be." The knowledge dawns on me as I say the words. "His magic kept us hostage, but now that he doesn't have it anymore..."

"Yes," says Franco. "We can choose. He can't even return to Earth as a cat without our years to do it."

"His time is up," says Val, finally smiling.

"I'll find a way back! I'll cut the bone off again somehow." He's trying to snarl, but his voice and face are drenched in fear. "You have no idea what I can do!"

"And look what we can do," says Franco, and he takes the soft orange ball of light in his hands, reaches his arms up, and sends it up into the gray sky.

"Thank you," he says as his body slowly fades away.

One by one, slowly at first and then with more power, the children all reach inside their own hearts, take their lights, and send them up. On. They fade from view slowly, but they all look happy while they do it.

Gozzelino runs around manically, looking for the book. "If I can't find a way to sever myself again, I'll release the demons. They'll devour everyone who's left!"

"Here we go, Mia," says Val from beside me, as if he hasn't heard Gozzelino at all. "I hope this works."

My heart starts to race. Do we all have to do this, too? All alone?

When his light-blue light hits the sky, it changes the color of the whole world. It's suddenly brighter and bluer, like the first day of spring.

"Hope I see you soon," he says to me just before he disappears.

"We have to, don't we?" asks Grace.

"I don't want to go alone," I say, "but I think we have to."

"I see it!" screeches Gozzelino. I whirl around, and he's pointing at me. Or, more accurately, he's pointing at my waist. Grace and I are the last two here. He starts running toward me, but I take the book and throw it like a frisbee, as far as I can, to the opposite side. If I can make myself do this, he'll have a choice, left here all alone: spend the afterlife in his own carnival, or open the book and be devoured like the beetle.

"Now seems like a good time," I say, making a joke because I'm actually really nervous again. "Okay, we can do this."

"We can," says Grace, already sending her purple orb up and fading away.

"All alone," I say, just as Gozzelino grabs the book in the distance.

"Mia, just go already."

I take my yellow light and send it up. I think I hear Gozzelino yell something again, but I'm not sure what it is. Now that I'm up here in Val's springtime sky, I feel pretty good. Proud of myself. Whole.

On.

What does it feel like to go on?

Is this it? I'd say it feels like air, but air is not this light. Neither is water. The concept of solid feels like an imaginary one. I am everywhere and nowhere.

I can see, though not the kind of sight with eyes: this is more like a feeling, some shapes, like shadows, but more detailed and from several angles at once.

What can I see?

Three figures lying on the ground with their arms wrapped around each other as if they've made some sort of promise. The world around us begins to come into view. We are under a bridge indeed, and mud mixed with sand is under us. We lie in between the bridge on one side and a broken, unused concrete construction barrier on the other. Gozzelino must have scouted this spot out before routing it to the portal because it's a tiny space, outdoors, still possible for someone to be found inside by the living, but hidden enough so that any accidental discovery would be highly unlikely. He probably meant for our bodies to rot right here. I don't know how we were sent back to our bodies, but I'm grateful we were because I would not have been able to find them on my own.

I can hear Grace's voice, though it's not the same as hearing with ears, and I can tell it's her even though it sounds nothing like her.

"Let's get back inside."

Do I even want to do that? This is such a beautiful feeling. What was on Earth, anyway?

Val's voice, which has that same ethereal quality, says, "I don't think I can."

Grace: "Keep trying. I'm going back now."

Beside me, Grace pulls herself together, like drops of light collecting themselves into a solid beam, and enters her body through her mouth. Val tries next, bringing himself together and heading for his own mouth. These bodies already look so foreign to me. Do I really want to go back inside?

Grace's body gasps and coughs, and she rolls over. She sputters and struggles and writhes, and I think about asking her to come back out again. It looks like more trouble than it's worth in there. She finally rolls over, looks at my face, and gives my shoulders a little shake.

"Come on, Mia," she says. I feel the vibrations running through the air as she says my name. "Mia. Come back."

Val is still trying. He must have given up on his mouth and is trying to get through an ear now. I want to help him, but I don't think I can.

"Mia!" calls Grace, this time with a slight tremor in her voice.

I have to get back, I know. With my parents treating me like a goldfish they just need to feed sometimes and her mother treating her like a project in need of rehabilitation, we need each other. We both need someone to really see us and love us for who we are, not who we will be. Not for what we can do, but for who we are when everything else is gone.

Val slows down and hovers above his body, a light that radiates a bit onto his grayish face.

"Remember your promise," he says at last.

His lifeless face and his ruined body tell the entire story. I don't know where he'll go from here. Does he stay, floating and watching but never returning? Does he leave this place entirely? Can he ever come back to visit? I don't know if he's wondering the same thing or not. I know that, right now, only one thing matters to him, anyway.

"I'll tell your mom," I say finally.

"Mia!" says Grace.

"You should get back," says Val.

I slowly pull myself together: it's like bringing out a magnet and feeling for metal. When my light is brightest, I float toward my mouth. My lips are purple and cold, but they warm up when I draw near. Grace's hand goes under my head. She's crying now.

"I'll see you later," I tell Val, and I will.

I go inside. I go back to life.

24

The floaty, underwater feeling doesn't last long after that, though I'm not sure how long it goes on. A minute? Twenty? Sixty? Some time later, I feel heaviness all around me, squeezing me and pressing down. It takes a moment for me to realize what has happened: I am back in my body. I am back.

My heavy eyes won't open, and my limbs won't move—how effortlessly I used to do both!—but I am alive on earth again, I'm certain. A revolting shock goes through me, and I convulse and cough. A happy scream erupts to my right, and Grace pulls me into a warm hug. I put my arms around her, too, and breathe her scent in—cool like peppermints. I was right. Those years still existed. With the Bone Carnival gone and Gozzelino stripped of his magic, they reverted back to her. Life seems like the kind of thing that can't quite be created or destroyed. I don't know about the first, but I know for sure now that the second is true.

Even though I've gone back to life being hard again, even though I feel heavy and broken and stiff, I am grateful to be back. I feel nothing but gratitude. I *am* gratitude.

"I thought you might not come back," Grace says, her breath warm against the back of my neck.

"You were here. How could I stay?" I hug her a little tighter, and she starts to cry, and then I do too. But it isn't because I'm sad. I'm crying because I am so happy. I never knew I could be this happy.

But our unbridled joy doesn't last long. She is the first to look down at Val.

"Val?" she says. She reaches out and touches his shoulders. "Val, come back."

"Grace," I whisper.

"Val!" she says, giving his shoulders a little shake now. "Val, it's okay, you can come back now."

Val's body looks a lot like it did at the Bone Carnival. His mussed, sandy-brown hair still falls around his head like a halo. His wrinkled tee shirt goes slightly up around his hips, and his superman underwear is visible at the waistline of his jeans. His jaw is slack and his eyes are lightly closed, like he's just taking a nap.

"I don't think he's coming back," I say. I reach out and take his hand, which is cold and stiff. Before this, I would have jerked away and that feeling would have haunted my nightmares. Now, I only remember my brave friend and what he did for us, for everyone. In Sunday school and camp, they're always talking about love and sacrifice, how people who love each other make sacrifices, but it doesn't mean it's fair. It doesn't mean it's good. I don't want Val's sacrifice; I want Val back.

177

Grace weeps more than I do. I put my arms around her as she cries and cries. "I'm sorry," she keeps saying to Val, over and over. "I'm sorry. I'm sorry."

Guilt crushes me. I want to be happy to be alive again, and I am, but I also feel like I don't deserve it if Val can't come back too. All he wanted to do was to see his Mom again. I didn't really understand that at the time, but now I realize how much his mom must have loved him for him to be brave like that for her. My mom and dad are going to be happy to see me. They love me, but not like this. I have a feeling it'll be the same with Grace's return.

"Come on," I tell Grace. "He wants his mom to know."

She buries her face in her hands. "We can't just leave him here."

"Then you stay with him," I say. "And I'll get help."

"You don't speak Italian," she says. "And I have no idea where we are. We could be way outside of Rome."

"I'll get help," I say. "I promise."

Before I can stumble to my feet, the light around us grows brighter and brighter, like a switch being slowly turned up until we are awash in golden light. Although I can't see them—or anything else, for that matter, in this brightness—I can feel them there. It's the kids from the carnival. They're all here.

"Thank you," says Franco.

"Thank you," say the girls.

"Thank you."

"Thank you."

I sit there, immersed in the light and the happiness of these souls and breathe in their peace. Beside me, Grace asks it like a question. "Val?"

178

We wait for his answer, but there is none. And soon, the chorus of "thank yous" fade away, and the lights separate from each other and float away like orbs in a fairy tale, away from us, and go above the bridge.

I never knew it was possible to feel so many feelings all at once: joy for those kids, relief for me and Grace, fear for Val. Each emotion is intense, and they all exist alongside each other as equals. But there's only one that needs something from me.

Grace nods, and I stumble to my feet, getting used to this heavy body again. Pain shoots through me, all around my soul. It takes effort to take one step, and then two. It takes effort to climb over the barrier. One step at a time, I struggle out from under the bridge. There's a busy road up above, drivers and cyclists hurry on by, totally unaware that up until a few minutes ago, they rode over the bodies of three dead kids beneath their tires.

My throat is dry. I have no idea how I'm going to do this, exactly, but I think about what I told Grace and Val in that tent: the hardest part is making yourself take the first action. I stand on the side of the road and wave my arms.

A cyclist catches my eye, and for the first time, I see from her face how pitiful I must look. Beneath her bright pink helmet, her face looks very concerned.

"*Posso aiutarla?*"

"I need help," I say in English.

She looks surprised, but then switches to English. "Yes, of course. What can I do?"

25

Fifteen minutes later, I am sitting on a stretcher under a space blanket with a bottle of water in my hands. Room temperature, of course. We're still in Italy, after all.

While the cyclist called the ambulance, I was able to confer with Grace briefly, and we agreed that our story would raise more questions than we were willing to answer, so we agreed on a set of facts that were not lies—we were kidnapped, we were dumped under this bridge, we don't remember it, we just woke up. When the paramedics rushed under the bridge, they whisked Grace and I away from Val at once and started doing CPR on his chest. Although I just caught a glimpse, it looked violent and harsh, and I wanted to tell them to cut that out, but Grace stopped me.

"This way they can tell his Mom they did all they could," she says. "He would have liked that."

I agreed with her, but I still can't stop my hands from shaking around the water bottle. There are a few cycles of them shouting and then growing silent again, and each time it makes me feel cold, small, and scared.

An officer who is directing traffic suddenly looks our way with an expression I can't read beneath his black sunglasses. He waves a black SUV toward us, and the door opens before it stops. Before anyone gets out, I know who it is.

"Mia!" says Mom, and she and dad get out. I want to stand, but I'm still feeling really shaky and unsteady, so I just set my water bottle down beside me. Grace clutches her blanket a little tighter to her throat while her mother runs to her too. Enzo is there too. The four of them have only us in their sights, and run toward us across the street.

Mom's hands are icy and thin, but she clutches my face. "You're alive," she murmurs.

My dad pats my back nervously. "We were kind of worried about you there," he says.

"It's safe to say you're grounded," she says and smiles slightly.

It's not right, their reaction. We've died and come back, but they're acting like I was lost in a department store. They're all nervous, all three of them. Only Enzo looks like he's maybe experiencing something real, but he's trying not to let it show: he's off to the side, looking at me with tears in his eyes and is holding his arms stiffly in the pocket of his hoodie.

Looking at them now, I feel like I'm having another out-of-body experience, only I'm very much here and inside my body now. *They're scared,* I realize. They've always been scared. Maybe they were scared for me, but I can finally see that that's not their main fear anymore. They're afraid of what people are thinking of them, all the time. I watch them with completely new eyes, the realization washing over me. Parents are just people, not perfect, not any better than us. They're just children who have grown up.

"You're grounded too, missy," says Dr. James, not even touching Grace.

I look at Grace. It's just like I said at the Bone Carnival: no one is coming to save us. But maybe that's okay. We don't get to choose our family we're born into, but maybe we can choose a different sort of family. Maybe we can make things better for each other.

Grace, as usual, understands what I'm trying and failing to put into words in my head. She just reaches out and squeezes my hand. In the background, a paramedic shout numbers in Italian, doing yet another round of CPR on Val. My mom looks from our hands to my face. I look back at her, really and truly unafraid at last. My fingers tighten around Grace's hand. Some things, I've learned, are worth the risk.

A frantic shout comes from under the bridge. Grace's eyes widen and her back bolts upright.

"A pulse," she says. "They've got a pulse on Val."

A pulse means a heartbeat. A heartbeat means...

I'm on my feet, scrambling down closer before anyone can stop me, Grace close at my heels. We ignore the shouts of the people who try to get us to come back, to stop, to sit down and drink our water and be good and stay out of the way. But they don't know what we went through to get here. They don't know what Val's return means to us.

They load Val's body onto a stretcher and put an oxygen mask over his face. In mere seconds, he is strapped and masked and rushed into the ambulance.

"Where are you taking him?" I ask a paramedic.

"Rome Memorial," she says in English.

"Mom," I call over my shoulder, "I need to go with him."

We don't have a car here, so I guess I'm asking her to call an Uber or something. But she gestures back to the black SUV she came in. The window rolls down, and it's none other than Signore Hairy Thumbs inside, his notebook tucked inside his front coat pocket. Seeing him again is like a punch to the gut, and it makes me feel like I did just a few days ago all over again: like a little girl in trouble. But his expression isn't scolding; it's determined.

"Get in," he says. "I'll take you all."

We wait in a frigid waiting room on green upholstered chairs with Italian talk shows blaring on TVs overhead. Grace and I sit together while Grace's mom and my mom try to talk about new ways to get us to come home. I think if we were in America, they'd want to examine us too, to make sure we were healthy, but in Italy they just assume if we're walking and talking, we're fine. Dad says the police have more questions for us, but it can wait. He and Enzo left together almost as soon as we arrived. But I'm staying right where I am until Val wakes up or...

I can't let myself think about the other option.

We're still waiting for Val's mom to come. It's apparently a long way from their small town to the city, and she's probably taking public transit all the way. That's the other thing I'm nervous about: I don't have much experience with mothers like her or relationships like this one. What could I possibly say to her? Would she want to know that even in death, Val thought about her, worried for her, wanted her to have closure and be happy? Or would she be happier to remember their time together and not have his memory talked over by two American strangers?

Our parents try hard to get us to come home, but in the end, Grace convinces them that we should at least wait until his mom arrives. I'm not budging, though, and if they want to make me, they can carry me out. Val was there for us when we needed him. Even though I have no idea what I'll say to his mom, I doubt he'd be very happy with us leaving his mother alone in a big-city hospital, waiting to hear whether her child will live or die. I think about Gozzelino's elixir and wonder if this was the feeling he was really trying to cure—this feeling of loss, of injustice, of fear, of helplessness in the living.

"How long was he missing?" I overhear one of the nurses asking another, both holding colorful water bottles that bounce against their legs as they walk through the waiting room. They must be from some English-speaking country, though not the US. They have accents. They must think nobody can understand them.

"Just over a week," she says. "Eight days."

"And the girls?" she asks, briefly looking over her shoulder at me.

"Two."

I sink deeper into the scratchy green chair and lean my head back. My soul and body are both so tired.

When Val's mother arrives, I know who she is the moment she walks through the glass doors. She and Val have the same sad eyes, the same pointed chin, the same plump cheeks. She speaks briefly to someone at the front desk, and they lead her down a hallway and through a set of double doors. I want to go with her, but instead, I just whisper the same word I whispered before. *Please,* I whisper. Grace looks up to where I'm looking, at the swinging doors where she's just passed through. *Please.*

The hospital only gets colder. Mom says we can't stay for much longer, but I tell her to just go if she wants to go. I'm staying here. I know now that the only thing that keeps her from dragging me out is the optics of hauling a recently-kidnapped middle schooler through the hospital. To be honest, she'd probably be fine, though in America they call the cops on moms just for leaving kids in the car in the Starbucks parking lot. Those are the parents she's afraid of, even though we're an entire day's plane ride away from them.

Finally, finally, a doctor comes in and walks toward me and Grace. We stand, though it's not easy, since I still feel sick.

"Are you the American friends of Valerius?" he asks in English.

"We are," I answer.

He smiles. "He's awake now."

I don't know why, but my hands are trembling as we walk down the hall and to his room. It's a wild thought, but I can't help but think there's been some mistake, and the doctor was really updating us about some other patient.

But when he leads us into his room, there's Val, lying in bed. His mother sits on the side of the bed stroking his hair. When we arrive, the doctor says something to her, and she gets up, walks over to us, cups my jaw in her warm hands, and kisses my forehead. And then she does the same to Grace.

She speaks Italian to us, but only Grace nods and says *grazie* back.

"Mia," croaks Val from bed. His mother rushes to his side and says something soothing.

"Hi, Val," I say. "We thought we'd lost you. How do you feel?"

He swallows hard. He's obviously weak, but I'm so glad to see he's here. He's going to make it.

He says something to me in Italian.

"I'm sorry," I say, "I can't—"

"He says he did it," says Grace quietly, coming over on the other side of the bed. "He did it even though he was scared, just like you said."

I realize that when we were in the Bone Carnival, we were in a death realm, so we could understand each other without language, just like the gladiators told us. Now that we're back, I won't be able to know what he's saying anymore.

He and Grace chat for a while in Italian, but I can tell by her face that even she's having trouble.

Eventually she gets up. His mom takes out her phone and puts in a phone number—Grace's, I guess. I look at Val fully in the face one more time.

He found a way back, and he didn't use fear, he was driven by love. It's something I can't understand, not right now, but I very much want to. At first, I feel a little lonely, and a little guilty. I don't know exactly what Val had to do to come back, but it looks like it was hard work, and I'm honestly not sure if I love my parents enough to do it. But maybe just because my parents don't love me like Val's mom loves him, it doesn't mean I am unworthy of love. It doesn't mean I have to be incapable of it too.

As we're leaving, I catch one more glimpse of Val and his mother, looking at each other, chatting like he's a child in a storybook just waking up in the morning, and she has nothing better to do than to just talk with him.

26

"No phone," my mom starts. "No TV. No seeing friends. No dessert for a month."

In our apartment, my dad fits my window with bars. He says it's to keep me safe, but I know they're really afraid of me running away again. Mom is sitting on my bed with me. I got myself ready for bed almost immediately after getting home. I cannot wait to sleep in a bed again. The sheets and pillows feel softer and cozier than ever before.

"Okay," I say. Punishments haven't bothered me for a long time—I know Mom and Dad will get tired of enforcing them after a few days anyway—but they bother me even less now. I'm stronger than I ever imagined myself to be. I led a full-blown rebellion of ghost children. I saved a dozen or more babies. I escaped an evil conjurer. Is it really supposed to bother me now that I can't have dessert?

"Mia!" Mom says and does her sharp exhale. "I don't think you know how serious this is."

CHAPTER 26

"No," I say, looking at her. "I don't think *you* know. I survived when I wasn't supposed to survive. If you're not going to be happy about that, you're not going to be happy at all, and if you're not going to be happy at all, why should I try anymore to make you happy?"

"Don't talk to your mother like that," mumbles Dad, looking for a loose screw on the floor.

Mom, though, looks stunned. "I *was* worried about you," she whispers.

I hold my breath and wait for her to continue.

"Do you know what I would have gone through? How it would have made me and your father look if you'd been killed?"

There it is. I want to fly off the handle and rage that she doesn't care about me, she only cares about herself. That's what the old Mia would do. I feel like the end of my childhood didn't happen in the Bone Carnival. It's happening right now. I don't think they can love me like I want them to—like I've seen parents love their kids in books or in movies, like I've longed for. I think there's some kind of block there. I think they can't.

And I don't know how to make that okay.

27

For the next week, I jump at the sight of every alley cat. I shiver at the music of every busker on the street. I "like" every instagram picture that Val posts, because just like I expected, I get my phone rights restored within a few days.

I sit in my Italian camp classes, feeling deflated until three o'clock, when we're done for the day, and spend the rest of the night sitting in front of my laptop, watching old movies. I don't want to go out. I don't feel like having any more adventures. I don't feel like myself anymore. I've heard from TV shows that people who have near-death experiences come back changed, and I wish that was it. I wish I'd just had the experience, and it was so shocking that I had trouble coming back. Instead, I feel disoriented because it has cast everything in my real life in sharp perspective. After going to such great lengths for others, it's harder for me to understand how they can be so completely into themselves. And then I keep thinking: What if Gozzelino was right? What if the unselfish thing to do really was to stay there in the Bone Carnival until he was done? Could he really have saved the entire human race from all sickness? Did I ruin that?

It sounds pretty on-brand for me. Is that why my parents are the way they are?

Grace's mom actually has stuck with her punishment, so we haven't seen much of each other outside of language camp, and even then, not much. She's in a different class than I am, so we can only really talk when we're waiting for them to pick us up at the end of the day.

One day, about two weeks after Val gets out of the hospital, the afternoon is extraordinarily hot. The sun beats down oppressively on the campus, and the walkways are vacant except for a handful of summer school students lazily making their way to their next class. Grace is there, staring off into the distance. I stand next to her and for a moment I can feel her there, slightly bigger than her body, cool like peppermint.

"You know," she says, "suddenly things that seemed important before just don't anymore."

"What do you mean?

"Being the best. It kind of makes me cringe now to admit this, but I just had to be the best in any group I was ever in. I felt like I just had to be the smartest, or the fastest, or the funniest." She turns to me, but she's still deep in thought. "It was almost uncontrollable; I just had to be number one. But none of that seems important at all anymore."

I nod. "I know what you mean. I guess I knew before that everybody dies, and that all of this," I gesture broadly at the lawn, both green under the trees

and sun-scorched brown everywhere else, "is tempo-
rary, but it's different now. But I've been thinking the
exact opposite."

"What do you mean?"

"I mean the things that didn't seem important to me
before seem really important now."

She frowns. "Like what?"

I take a deep breath in through my nose. "I mean
my mom. I just kind of took for granted that she loved
me, but she doesn't—not in the way I want her to. My
dad too, but he's different. And now that we've died
and come back, I'm thinking that it's not that she
doesn't love me; it's that she can't."

Grace presses her lips together and nods slowly.
"Mia, do you know what a personality disorder is?"

"No."

"My therapist told me about them. I think my mom
has one. It's a real thing—people think they deserve
special treatment. They really think they're better than
other people, they can't think about themselves in any
else's situation, and they don't do relationships well.
Most of how they relate to other people is just about
making themselves feel better."

It's like a puzzle is coming together in my head.
How many times has my mom told me not to embarrass her? How many times have I gotten in trouble
because she was afraid I'd ruin her reputation? How
many times has she gotten mad at me because I failed
to read her mind and meet the needs she didn't tell
me about and was angry I wasn't thinking of her
all the time?

"Wait," I say, "she still does things with me some-times. We always bake cookies together at Christmas."

"Does she Instagram it?"

"Well, yeah."

"Have you ever had fun with her—or your dad, for that matter—without them taking a picture?"

Her quiet tone and raised eyebrow makes me sure she knows the answer is no, which is good because I am too shocked to speak.

"I didn't think so." She turns back, surveying the lawn, adjusting her backpack. "But it's okay, Mia. My therapist is always saying that the way other people treat you isn't your fault, but I didn't understand that until now. I think me trying to be the best at everything was just me trying to get Mom to finally come around and see that I'm a good daughter. I'm not interested in that anymore."

I feel like I've just been punched in the gut. "How is it okay?"

"I don't really know," she admits. "I guess it really isn't. But I don't want to do that anymore—I mean, try to earn her love. It might not even be possible. I mean, look at Gozzelino. Look at what he was willing to do to impress his mom. And she was already dead! He was just doing that to himself, but he was hurting a lot of other people in the process."

As she speaks, I prod my loose tooth with the tip of my tongue. It's been a game lately; it feels like it's hanging on by a string. Which, I suppose, it kind of is. But just as she finishes talking about Gozzelino, it surprises me by popping out. It lands on my tongue, and I rush to spit it out. There's no blood, just the molar, looking much smaller in my hand than it felt in my mouth.

I hold it out triumphantly to Grace. "Look!"

She looks down and laughs. "Gross. And congratulations."

I flash a giant smile. "How do I look?"

"Even better than usual."

Now it's my turn to laugh. "Maybe I'll put it under my pillow tonight. I'm not so sure the tooth fairy is fiction anymore."

"I know what you mean. Like, what else don't we know?"

"So many possibilities."

I put the tooth in my pocket and instead of taking my hand out, I roll it in between my fingers. I can't believe it's this small. Maybe I'll put it under my pillow, after all. Why not?

"So," I say, "do you have to go to, like, a doctor to know if you have personality disorder?"

"Ugh, just google it. Don't make me think any-more today."

Not the answer I was expecting. I feel like the old Grace not only would have told me, but would make me feel dumb for not knowing. If something really is off with our moms, though, this is probably the best we can both do—be kind. Be understanding. Not pass along pain to other people just because our par-ents hurt us.

"And I don't really know if your mom has it," she adds. "You know what would be a good test? Ask her about it. People with personality disorders would never admit that there's even a small possibility they have one. If she gets mad and tells you that maybe you're the one who's sick, there's a good chance she does." Just then, her mom rounds the corner and waves to her daughter, gesturing for her to join her so she doesn't have to walk all the way across the quad. Grace slips her other arm through her backpack. "See you tomorrow, Mia. Oh, and I forgot!"

"What?"

"Val and I have been emailing back and forth, when I can get on the library computers. He wants to know if you and I can come to his house some time before the end of the summer."

"Oh," I say, "I don't know."

"I think if your parents said yes, my mom would let me go. That's our only shot, I think. Work on them."

"Okay."

When Enzo gets out of class, he and I walk back to the apartment together. In these few weeks, we've mostly talked about class that day or interesting things we see or good food we want to try, but today I want to talk about something that matters.

"Enzo?" I ask as we round a corner and see a crumbling column. We don't know if it's really old or if it's a cheap replica. People sit around it, texting and eating fries. "What did you think when I was gone?"

"I was hoping you'd be back before Mom and Dad tried for a replacement baby."

"Funny," I say, "but I'm serious."

"Seriously?" he asks, his tone softening and his pace slowing. "I was really scared. Mom and Dad kept telling me you'd run away, but when you didn't come back the second night, I was majorly freaked. I knew you'd been kidnapped, but nobody believed me. When we pulled up to the bridge, and I saw you standing there, I felt like it was the luckiest we'd ever get in our lives."

It's the most sincere thing I'd ever heard from him, and all it took was me asking. "Why didn't you tell me before?"

He bites his lip, looking embarrassed. "I don't know. I wanted to, but it just never seemed like a good time. But you can talk to me about it, if you want. You do seem different now."

"I am different now," I admit. "I don't think I can talk about what happened yet, but maybe someday."

We told the police that someone took us when we were walking through the graveyard and got caught in the rain. Both of us described Gozzelino, and the police did a sketch. With no power remaining to come back to this world, even as a cat, they'll be looking for him for a long time.

"I get it," he says, but of course he doesn't. How could he?

At our apartment, I find Mom hunched over her computer, eyes moving while she reads something on the screen.

"Mom?"

"Not now, Mia."

I have the urge to do something ostentatious, like walking up and snapping her laptop shut, but I just take a breath. "I need to talk to you."

"Can it wait?"

"No."

"Okay," she says sarcastically, looking up over her screen with lidded eyes, "what is so important that it cannot wait until after I have responded to this student asking for an emergency extension due to a death in the family?"

I take one more breath. And then I'm hit with a sudden burst of inspiration. "What are you writing him?"

"I am writing to say that the syllabus clearly says when assignments are due and that I can't make exceptions."

"But can't you put yourself in his shoes? Especially after what just happened to me?"

"I cannot," she says, bringing her eyes back to the screen, "and you're not dead."

I feel like I just got the answer to my question, but now I don't know what to do with it. I mean, it's not like I can move out. And Grace said she was actually happier when she stopped trying to change her mom, so I don't know if changing her is even possible. All those times I finally had her attention—they'd all come at the cost of me doing something outrageous and getting in trouble. I don't know if I'm quite done with trouble— technically I can't be, if she's right and I really am a magnet for it—but I'd rather be in trouble for my good reasons, instead of using it to get her to talk to me.

With that in mind, I make one more small attempt: "I lost my tooth today."

"I thought you'd lost them all already."

"No. This is my last one."

"Well. Just don't expect the tooth fairy to come this late."

I turn to leave without another word, but not because I'm mad. It's just because I'm ready to stop expecting things to happen that just can't.

28

That night, I dream I'm back in a tent with Val and Grace. We're all surprised to see each other, and there is a brief moment of collective panic before Grace suggests this might be just a dream. When she says this, I remember everything—that we all escaped the Bone Carnival, that the souls of the other children went on, and that the three of us made it back to our bodies to live the rest of our lives in peace. I realize that she has to be right; this must be a dream because I remember going to sleep just a few hours ago in my bedroom in Rome.

We decide to go out to explore, but when we open the tent flap, we are bombarded with iridescent light. Colors swirl before my eyes, and I am enchanted at the beauty. A moment later, voices speak to us. They sound like the kids we just left.

"Stay with each other," they say in chorus.

"Stay with each other?" I ask. "What do you mean? Is Gozzelino still a threat?"

"He cannot touch you now," one answers. "But he knows that others can. Stay close, and protect each other."

As the voices fade into silence, Val turns to me and shrugs. "We can stay close. My mom makes really good gnocchi, Mia. You can come over on Friday. My mom says your whole family can come."

"My mom says she'll let me come if your family goes," says Grace.

"I don't want to ask her," I say. "I'm afraid."

The dream transforms.

I'm in the kitchen at home in Louisville, making Christmas cookies with Mom.

"We're out of dough," I tell her.

"That's okay," she says. And then she reaches into my chest and pulls out my heart. She takes it in her hands, kneads it, douses it in flour, flattens it with a rolling pin. She takes a cookie cutter and presses it into the red substance on the counter. She takes the shape she's made and puts it on a sheet alongside the bells, trees, and angels. And then she takes a picture.

When I wake in the morning, I have the urge to go find Enzo and tell him all about the dreams. Instead, I stay in bed and look out the window, watching the sweet-white clouds move slowly across the sky above the buildings. With each passing minute, I feel better. I was always a little afraid of growing up, but now that it's happening, I know I can do it.

Enzo and I ask Mom and Dad about going to Val's, and they give us an entire Saturday to ourselves. They talk with Enzo sternly the night before, telling him to keep eyes on the two of us the entire time without exception, and he acts differently than he did before. Before, he would have sulked and rolled his eyes. Now, he assures them with rapt attention that he will and that we'll all be safe.

On the way to the subway station, Val pulls out his phone again and starts texting. "Don't worry," he says, "I'm just letting Erin know I won't be available today."

I shift my gaze from the shops we're passing to his face. "Erin? Who's Erin?"

"Erin is my girlfriend," he says calmly.

"You don't have a girlfriend!"

"We've been dating for about four months," he says, slipping his phone into his pocket. He hops up onto the curb and turns his back to outside of the bus station. "You're the only one who knows. And I think Dad might too. I sometimes see him checking my phone."

Dad does that sometimes to my phone too. "Has he said anything?"

"Nah. I think he's waiting for me to tell him. I might, before we leave." He looks around and suddenly, with his sunglasses and his hands in his pockets, he looks unthinkably cool. Is this how Erin sees him? What does she look like?

"When do we get to meet her?" I ask.

"I'm not sure. She and I may go to different colleges next year."

He suddenly looks really sad, and I want to help but don't know how. But then he kicks a piece of trash on the ground and turns to me.

"Mia," he says, "remember my big fight with Mom?"

"What big fight?" asks a voice from behind us. Grace is standing there, with a cross-body bag slung over her, with a hand resting on top. I expect Enzo to shut down and stop talking about it, but he surprises me. He turns, sighs, and tells her.

"Our family had kind of an all-out brawl just before we came here. It started with just me and Mom, but then Mia and Dad got involved and all this stuff that we never talked about before just kind of..."

"Exploded," I finish. Hearing him talk about this now stirs something in my heart. It feels so good to know for sure I wasn't making this up.

"Mom wanted me to go to the university where she and Dad work—she'd already told all her friends I was going there—but I really want to go to a smaller one, farther away. I'd put off making a commitment for long enough, so I went ahead and told the smaller college I was coming."

"She lost her mind," I tell him, remembering. She started by telling Enzo they wouldn't pay for it, and Enzo told her he'd take out loans. She told him he was not allowed to make these kinds of decisions for himself. She said since we had the same last name, we were obligated not to do anything that would embarrass her. Then she brought me into it.

"Mom started talking about how she'd expect this kind of thing from Mia, but not from me."

"She said that I was always doing stuff to embarrass her and that I was a bad influence on Enzo," I say, remembering and feeling that same shame sweep my body. It felt like I'd never be enough for her, like I'd been disappointing her every minute of every day and not realizing it.

But that night, Enzo came to my defense. He told her she wasn't being fair. He told her to leave me out of it. And she wasn't used to being challenged.

She started screaming. Enzo screamed back, and I did too. Dad tried to calm us all down, but ended up in the din with the rest of us, and we all went after each other—parents against kids—until my throat burned. Enzo said he'd go to his friends and tell them about his control-freak parents, and Mom laughed.

"Do you think they'll believe you?" she asked. Her voice was ragged. "My Instagram is full of pictures of you getting every little thing you want. Pictures of all of us going out and having fun. Pictures of us as a happy family. And we are. As long as you do what I tell you, we'll always be a happy family. Nobody will believe your story when there's so much evidence you're making it all up."

"And nobody would believe anything else," I add quietly.

Grace stands there, looking at the ground. Going through all of this kind of makes me feel like I've just puked up something nasty—terrible in the moment, but now that it's out there, I feel great. I glance at Enzo, and he gives me a little smile and a little nod. We may not be able to escape, but it's real—it happened—and we both know it.

"So," says Enzo. "All that to say that I have no idea when you'll meet Erin, and I still don't actually know where I'm going to college next year."

Grace reaches in her purse for her phone. "You know what I think you'd both really like? Therapy." She taps the screen. "I'm sending you the name of my therapist now. You can talk to him online too."

Enzo reaches down to pinch a discarded candy bar wrapper and toss it into one of those weird street trash cans. "Has it helped you?"

"Yeah. I think it'd help you too. You're right; it's good to talk about problems we wish weren't problems."

After the bus and train ride, Val meets us at the terminal, looking much better than he did at the hospital. He's still thinner than I remember from the carnival, but his smile is warmer, his eyes more animated. Grace reaches out her arms and they hug, greeting each other in his language. I hug him too, and he says, "Hello, how are you?" but no more. I say a few things I've learned at language camp, and he responds politely, using words he knows I'll understand. "How are you?" "Fine, how are you?" It doesn't seem to matter as much as it did before. The language is still a barrier, but not an insurmountable one. We're still laughing and hugging and happy to see each other.

We walk the three miles back to his home, Enzo and Grace translating for me as he tells us about his recovery. He says every adult he knows has done nothing but cook, clean, and cook some more for him since he's been back. And his friends have secured a TV for him and hooked it up in his bedroom so he can watch the matches even as he rests. It's all so different than the way Grace and I have experienced the past two weeks—we were just kind of thrown back into normal life before, as if our journey past death was an inconvenient blip in the itinerary. But then again, Val was dead longer than we were.

"Welcome home!" he says in English, gesturing at a house in the distance.

It's two stories and made in brown stucco, and the texture makes it look a little like a storybook house of chocolate icing. The roof is a more reddish color, and there's a wrought-iron fence on the balcony below. On one side of the house, a sprawling garden reaches toward the sun. The front door is wide open, and a bright white chicken wanders out into the yard, joining several others.

He says something and they all laugh. Grace translates: Val's mother never liked killing the chickens for dinner as a girl, so she and Val are vegetarians now. Where most people see entrees, they see pets.

A gravel walkway leads us to the open front door, and mouth-watering scents get stronger and stronger: garlic, tomatoes, salt, basil, and others blend together in a pleasant combination that makes me feel snug and warm all the way down to my toes.

"Mama!" shouts Val, and the little woman appears in the doorway in a grayish apron and her hair in a knot on top of her head. She smiles and waves us in.

I've never had a better meal in my life. Gnocchi, as it turns out, are little balls of potato, rolled and formed into tiny, flavorful pillows. Her red sauce is sweet and earthy, like she's grown the steaming pot in the garden and brought it into the kitchen. We have crisp salad, which feels zesty and full of life, homemade bread, warm and tender, and for dessert, more lemon pound cake, this kind richer and more pungent than the one I got from the bakery in Rome.

"Ask him how everything is so good," I tell Enzo, and he obliges.

Enzo listens intently to Val's mother, and then tells me, "She says she started making this meal months ago, when she planted the seeds in the garden. She says food is life, and it never ends, but this is her favorite stage."

I'm not quite sure what to make of that. But we eat and I keep eating long after my belly is full. Afterwards, we all help clean up. Enzo and Val's mother have coffee at the table, and Grace and Val and I go out to the garden to pick some oranges to take home.

Val reaches up and plucks one off the branch, and tells Grace something. Grace looks stricken.

"What?" I ask urgently.

"He says he had a dream last night."

I blink, but somehow I'm not as surprised as I should be. Pieces of the first dream come back to my memory, and from the way they're both looking at me, I can already tell what's happening. "Were you at the carnival too?"

They nod.

Grace answers slowly, as if she's trying to remember. "They came back to thank us. They told us we'd be okay."

"And they told us to stick by each other."

Val hands me the orange, and it feels heavy and cool in my hands. I know without having to ask that they did not have the second dream—that one was just mine. I can't change the circumstances I was born into, but I can change my remaining years I've fought to take back.

The thing I love about that movie, *Roman Holiday*, is that it doesn't have a happy ending. In other stories, the characters are simply whisked away from their bad situations—the girl marries a handsome prince, or the boy gets an invitation to a magical school, or the siblings are adopted by a benevolent and rich caregiver. *Roman Holiday* isn't like that. The princess falls in love with a commoner, but it doesn't work. They go back and face the lives they were given. Even if what you want is a good thing to want—romance, or a noble cause for the world, or just love from your parents—that doesn't mean you always get to have it.

Nobody is coming to save me. But that's okay—I can find others who are in the same mess. I'm a magnet for those.

THE END

DISCUSSION QUESTIONS

1. Consider the title: BONE CARNIVAL. What does each individual word remind you of? What can you guess about the book by putting the words together?

2. Mia's relationship with both Grace and Val begins poorly. Is it possible to have a close friendship with someone even if you don't make a good first impression? How do you know?

3. Would you consider Mia to be a good role model for kids? Why or why not?

4. Who is the bravest character in the book? What makes you think this?

5. When Grace is taken into the Bone Carnival, Mia jumps in after her. Do you think she should have done this? What do you think would have happened if she'd chosen to walk away?

6. Which character reminds you most of yourself? Why?

7. What does Mia accept about her family at the end of the book? What does she accept about herself? Is one of these easier than the other?

ACKNOWLEDGEMENTS

In the course of writing this book, major changes were rocking my world. Bringing Mia's story onto the page was a way to hold onto some semblance of sanity and channel all of my confusion and uncertainty into something meaningful. In March 2020, I was a few chapters in, having followed my agent's suggestion that I write something with a "creepy carnival vibe" when the pandemic changed everything for everyone.

Within two years, I had two babies, moved twice, homeschooled our kids, earned my MFA, supported my husband as he sold our brick-and-mortar business, and finished this book. I did none of this alone, and my gratitude for those who held my hand throughout this time, both literally and figuratively, is deeper than words can express, but I'll try.

Ryan, you're my perfect partner. Your faith in me and in God's vision for our lives keeps me going when I want to give up. Thank you for showing me what unconditional love looks like and for being the rock in our family.

To Finnegan, Clark, Wilder, and Reese Noelle: your love of stories and willingness to go adventuring with me and your dad are gifts that neither of us take for granted. I love you so much, and I'll never stop trying to be the best mother I can be for you.

To the Hamline MFAC faculty, especially Coe Booth, Claire Rudolpf-Murphy, Elana K. Arnold, Sherri Smith, Erin Entrada Kelly, Swathi Avasthi, Brandy Colbert, Jackie Briggs-Martin, and Lisa Jahn-Clough. Thank you for your generosity and for giving me the feedback I needed to solidify this story.

To Anne Ursu, my teacher and mentor and—I literally cannot believe I get to say this—friend. Your books moved me to take risks when I have something important to say, but your spirit inspires me to be playful and curious while I'm doing it. If I get to pass along even half of the knowledge and encouragement and wisdom you've given me, I'll consider myself lucky.

To T.A. Barron, your vote of confidence in me as a writer came at the moment I needed it most. I'll never forget it. Thank you for being an uplifting force for good in the world.

To my critique partners and writing groups, the Llama Squad, the Misfits, and the Athenas: Angela Cowen, Em Shotwell, E.J. Wenstrom, Catherine Bakewell, Sabrina

Kleckner, Marina Hill, Miep, Katy Lapierre, Sarah Jane Pounds, Lillie Vale, Katie Knightly, Aurora Matrinez, Makayla Sophia, C.T. Danford, Sarah Fowerbaugh, Gabriela Romero Lacruz, Ashley McAnelly, Rochele Smit, Cyla Panin, Melissa Bowers, Lenore Stutz, Lisa Matlin, Rachel, Jania Johnson, Erin Madison, Katherine Holom, Nicole Aronis, and Mary Roach. There's a special place for each one of you in my heart, and your unfailing support has meant the world to me.

To the team at OBP, especially Arielle Haughee: thank you for your trust in me, and for your vision to bring *Bone Carnival* into the world. I am absolutely thrilled to have had this book edited and published by you.

ABOUT
THE AUTHOR

Megan Lynch is a middle school teacher, poet, and award-winning novelist. She earned her MFA in creative writing for children and young adults from Hamline University in 2022 and continues to look for opportunities to learn a little more each day. Megan enjoys spending time with her family at home in Nashville, Tennessee.